Blotto, Twinks and the Conquistadors' Gold

Simon Brett

CONSTABLE

CONSTABLE

First published in Great Britain by Constable in 2023

ISBN: 978-1-40871-655-7

Typeset in Palatino by Photoprint, Torquay
Printed and bound in Great Britain by Clays Ltd, Elcograf S.p.A.

Papers used by Constable are from well-managed forests and
other responsible sources.

MIX
Paper from
responsible sources
FSC
www.fsc.org   FSC® C104740

Constable
An imprint of
Little, Brown Book Group
Carmelite House
50 Victoria Embankment
London EC4Y 0DZ

An Hachette UK Company
www.hachette.co.uk

www.littlebrown.co.uk

Blotto, Twinks and
the Conquistadors' Gold

Also by Simon Brett

To my sister, Penny.
With love

1

Blotto Alone

Blotto without Twinks was rather like a referee's whistle without a pea in it. Though he had everything the younger son of a Duke could wish for at his home, Tawcester Towers – hunting on his magnificent charger Mephistopheles, trips out in his Lagonda to knock vicars off bicycles in the narrow lanes of Tawcestershire – he still missed his sister.

From childhood, except when Blotto was away at Eton, the siblings had rarely been apart for any length of time. Their solidarity had been useful in dealing with the idiocies of Loofah, their older brother and current Duke of Tawcester. More importantly, a united front had helped them stand up against the ferocious will of their mother, the Dowager Duchess, to whom the most forbidding North Face of any mountain in the world would lose out in the Implacability Stakes.

A rueful Blotto remembered in precise detail when his sister had first broached the subject of their forthcoming separation. After a successful day in the hunting field, which had destroyed many yards of the local farmers' fences and caused a serious diminution in the Tawcestershire fox population, Blotto was drinking cocoa in the white lace and silk fluffiness of Twinks's boudoir when she made her announcement.

'Blotto me old carriage crankshaft, you know I have recently rather pitched the crud into the custard so far as the Mater's concerned . . . ?'

'No,' he said. Except in matters concerning cricket or hunting, Blotto could be unobservant about what was going on around him. He was blithely unaware of atmospheres between people. He certainly hadn't noticed that the '*froideur*' between his sister and mother was any '*froider*' than usual.

'Well, not to fiddle round the fir trees, brother of mine, the Mater was very keen to get me to twiddle the old marital reef-knot with the Earl of Minchinhampton . . .'

'Who?'

'Niffy Nottsborough.'

'Ah. On the same page now.' The nickname clarified things. Blotto had actually been at Eton with the aforementioned Niffy Nottsborough.

'The Mater was particularly on the mustard because the Earl of Minchinhampton is the son of the Duke of Thetford and, when the old gargoyle takes a one-way ticket to the Pearlies, Niffy will inherit the title.'

'Will he, by Denzil!'

'Of course he will, Blotters. As you've known since you were in nursery-naps, that's how primogeniture works.'

'Tickey-tockey,' said Blotto with some uncertainty. He never felt entirely comfortable around long words, and he knew that those with 'genit' in them could be rather rude.

'Anyway, the Mater's gone into a right stick-in-a-wasp's-nest about my refusing to ding the church bells with Niffy.'

'Toad-in-the-hole!' said Blotto. But he wasn't really surprised. The Dowager Duchess's reactions to having her will thwarted made the eruption of Krakatoa look like a

2

minor movement in a molehill. 'So, if I may pose the questionette, sister of mine . . . why did you turn the poor pineapple down?'

'Niffy? I turned him down because he has the looks of a frog keen to return to tadpole status . . . because the material between his ears is pure unadulterated kapok . . . because his conversation rarely aspires to the level of the averagely gifted two-year-old . . . and, worst of all, because he once had the brazen gall to say to me "Don't you worry your pretty little head about that" . . .'

'All black marks in the copybook, Twinks, I can see that.'

'And also,' she concluded witheringly, 'when a boddo gets the nickname "Niffy", it's usually for a reason.'

'You're bong on the nose there. At Eton his study was known as "The Pong Room at Lord's". And in chapel, Niffy always had to sit in his own pew.'

'Anyway, Blotters, to escape the phosphorescent fury of the Mater's wrath, I was thinking of pongling away from Tawcester Towers for a breakette.'

'Visiting one of your debby chumbos in the Metrop, eh?'

'No, Blotters, further afield than that.'

'Then where, in the name of strawberries?' asked Blotto, for whom stirring anywhere off the Tawcester Towers estate was an act of impetuous folly.

'Mexico,' came the cool reply.

'Mexico! But that's . . . that's . . .' Geography not being one of his strengths, he concluded lamely, '. . . a long way away. And it's abroad! Why would anyone with half a braincell want to go abroad?'

'To escape the wrath of the Mater?'

'Ah, yes. You've pinged a partridge there. But surely that's not the whole clangdumble?'

So, Twinks had explained in more detail the reason for her travels. One of the few people she knew at her own intellectual level was a certain Professor Erasmus

3

Holofernes. He lived and worked at the all-male post-graduate Oxford college, St Raphael's. And one of his fellow academics, Professor Hector Troon-Wheatley, an expert on the civilisation of the Aztecs, had recently gone out to Mexico to examine an exciting new archaeological find there in a site called the Attututulluoo Caves. Twinks, who had had a lifelong fascination with all things Aztec and who knew as much on the subject as most experts, would be the perfect assistant for Troon-Wheatley on the trip.

Another attraction for her was the opportunity to visit a friend, Begonia Guiteras, whom Twinks had met while the Mexican was doing the London season as a means of learning English. The two beautiful and independent young women had hit it off. They longed to spend more time together. And, serendipitously, it turned out that Begonia lived in the province of Jalapeno, virtually on the doorstep of the Aztec dig.

Her father, General Henriquez Guiteras, had extensive estates in the area and was deeply involved in local politics. Staying with the family, Twinks would be able to mix her archaeological business with the pleasure of Begonia's company.

It was the perfect way of escaping the fulminating recriminations of the Dowager Duchess. Twinks was ecstatic about the prospect.

Blotto less so.

A surprising effect of his loneliness was that, in his sister's absence, Blotto spent more time in London. Though the Tawcester Towers estates contained everything he could ever wish for in terms of activities, it wasn't so well stocked for company. He rarely saw his brother or mother. Loofah lived in a separate wing, corralled by his wife

4

Sloggo and miscellaneous daughters. And avoiding the Dowager Duchess in her domain of the Blue Morning Room was, for Blotto, a daily preoccupation.

His only kindred spirit on the premises was the chauffeur Corky Froggett, but he found that even the pleasures of discussing the Lagonda's fine engineering were finite.

At least in London, a bereft Blotto could spend time at his club, The Grenadier (known to all its members as 'The Gren'). There, in the company of various old muffin-toasters from Eton, he could get mournfully wobbulated.

So low was his general mood that sometimes he didn't drive the Lagonda to London himself but let Corky Froggett do it. The barometer of Blotto's feelings had moved that far from its default setting of 'Sunny'. He had even been heard on occasion to utter that expression bordering on despair, 'Broken biscuits!'

He was in The Gren late one morning, working his way morosely down a bottle of the Club Claret when he was greeted by a hearty, 'Blotto, me old soup-strainer! How're your doodles dangling?'

The speaker turned out to be Willy 'Ruffo' Walberswick, a fellow Old Etonian, who had subsequently rather downgraded himself from the aristocracy by becoming a journalist.

Having assured the new arrival (possibly inaccurately) that his doodles were dangling in parade-ground order, Blotto offered Ruffo a drink.

'You're a gent, me old duffel coat. I'll have a brandy and s – light on the s, though. Need a good few bracers over the next twenty-four hours before I pongle down to Southampton. Boat to catch tomorrow night. Off to the latest international incident.'

'So, Ruffo, to dot the tees and cross the eyes, what do you mean by an "international incident"?'

'I mean the next powder keg on a very short fuse, set shortly to spoffing well detonate with an impact that'll coffinate thousands.'

'Oh, and where is this particular powder keg when it's got its spats on?' asked Blotto without much interest. International incidents were low on his scale of priorities, only marginally above ladies' fashions and royal romance. Assassinations and revolutions would never attain the allure of hunting or cricket.

But he became more concerned when Ruffo replied, 'Mexico.'

'Mexico? What's put lumps in the custard there?'

'Could be another revolution,' said Ruffo. 'Boss of one of the provinces has declared it an independent republic, with himself as its tin-pot dictator!'

'Which province?' asked Blotto, though he only knew the name of one.

And sure enough, that was the answer Ruffo gave: 'Jalapeno.'

'So, what's the name of this tin-pot dictator?'

He kind of knew what the answer would be.

'General Henriquez Guiteras,' Ruffo announced.

'Of course, I will do whatever it is Your Lordship requires of me,' said Corky Froggett. 'And if the duty necessitated my laying down my life in your defence, I would regard that as a generous bonus.'

'Toad-in-the-hole, Corky! You always were a Grade A foundation stone!'

'Thank you, milord,' said the humbly gratified chauffeur. 'You said the excursion would involve "abroad". If I may ask ... which country where the natives have grown up without the advantage of being British are we due to visit this time?'

'Mexico,' the young master replied. Now that he knew his sister was staying in a country that was the next 'powder keg on a very short fuse, set shortly to spoffing well detonate with an impact that'll coffinate thousands', he thought he should pongle off and check on the well-being of the young shrimplet.

Corky Froggett was unfazed by the news of their destination. 'And do you know much about that country, milord?'

'A boddo like me doesn't need to know much about a country, Corky. Foreign countries are all as alike as two peas in a whistle. They're "abroad" and that's all there is to it. The only thing you need to know about an abroad country is whether they play cricket or not.'

'And do the Mexicans play cricket, milord?'

'I haven't got a tinker's inkling, Corky. But I do know that a lot of the African countries are a bit slow off the chocks when it comes to cricket.'

'Erm ... milord.' The chauffeur negotiated his passage carefully. 'I don't believe Mexico is in Africa.'

'Rats in a sandwich! Where have they put the fumacious place then? Asia?'

'I believe the country is in the south of America, milord.'

'Is it? Dashed peculiar the places people put things. And you don't know whether the boddoes there play cricket or not?'

'I would think the chances are rather against it, milord.'

'Never mind. I'll teach them. Make sure my bat's packed in the back of the Lag.'

'Oh? We'll be taking the Lagonda with us, will we, milord?'

'Is the King German? Of course we will, Corky. So, get the old bird up to her sprucely best.'

'The Lagonda is always in perfect condition, milord.' The chauffeur would have been angry, had anyone other than the young master made the insinuation. 'Engine tuned as finely as a Stradivarius.'

Neither Corky nor Blotto knew what a Stradivarius was (though Blotto thought it might be a motorcycle), but they had both heard the expression used and taken a fancy to it.

'And may I ask, milord,' the chauffeur continued, 'when we will be setting off on this expedition?'

'This afternoon,' the young master replied. 'Catching a boat that leaves Southampton at ten pip emma. Why, Corky, is that putting too much skiddle under your skink?'

'Of course not, milord. I am always ready for any service Your Lordship may require of me.'

'Good ticket, Corky.' Blotto moved away from the garage. 'I'll get my man to trundle some trews into a trunk and we'll be off in . . . what, half an hour?'

'Perfect, milord.'

'So, we'd better both tick off our to-dos.'

'Very good, milord.'

Apart from packing, the chauffeur's main 'to-do' was breaking to one of the under-housemaids, for whom he had developed a *tendresse*, the news that he was about to leave for an unspecified length of time on a dangerous, and possibly fatal, mission to Mexico.

Blotto's 'to-do' involved imparting the same information, first to his hunter Mephistopheles, who was always very understanding about his master's excursions. And next to his mother, whose reactions to such news were less predictable.

'Why, Blotto,' the Dowager Duchess of Tawcester's voice rumbled, 'do you tell me this in a manner which suggests it might be of interest to me?'

'Well, Mater, I just thought I shouldn't pongle off to Mexico without sending you a semaphore on the subj.'

'Blotto, do you think that your presence or absence at Tawcester Towers in any way affects my daily life?'

'Well, maybe just a widge.'

'Not even the smallest shaving of a widge fallen from a widge-maker's bench, Blotto.'

'Ah. Right. Well. If that's the way the carpet's unrolling, then . . . hoopee-doopee!'

'You should have got it into your thick skull by now, Blotto, that you have never been of any interest to me, and you never will be of any interest to me, unless your elder brother Loofah gets a one-way ticket to the family vault . . .'

'Bong on the nose, Mater.'

'. . . in which case we would face the unappetising prospect of having you installed as Duke of Tawcester.'

'Tickey-tockey!'

'The one thing I should remind you of, Blotto, on your foreign travels . . .'

'Yes, Mater?'

'. . . as ever, if you see an opportunity to bring money back with you, or to make money in any way, take it. The Tawcester Towers plumbing is, as always, in serious need of repair.'

'Yes, Mater. *Any* way of making money?'

'Isn't that what I just said, Blotto?' the Dowager Duchess thundered. 'Oh, and if making money involves marrying a foreign heiress, that's splendid. With the usual proviso . . . that you stay married to her out wherever you find her. Don't think of bringing anyone like that back here.'

'Very good, Mater.'

'Now, Blotto, leave the Blue Morning Room! One of the advantages of living in a home as generously proportioned as Tawcester Towers is that whole months can go by without our paths crossing. My day is never improved by the sight of you in it.'

In common with the rest of her class, the Dowager Duchess did not believe in showing too much softness in the upbringing of children.

2

Crossing the Pond

Neither Blotto nor Corky regarded travel as pleasurable in its own right. It was a means of reaching a destination. And, though there might be splendid sights to be seen on the way, nothing could shake their conviction that better views were available back in the Land of Golden Lions. Particularly, back at Tawcester Towers.

What travelling they did do, they liked to do as much as possible under their own steam. Sadly, the Lagonda could not supply the right kind of steam for a crossing of the Atlantic, so for that they had to rely on an ocean liner. But they spent the minimum time they could on shipboard. Never even considering a sea voyage down to Veracruz or another Mexican port, their plan involved crossing from Portsmouth to New York and driving themselves from there to their destination.

Before they left, in consultation with Blotto, Corky had loaded the Lagonda's luggage compartment with items that might be necessary on their journey. Spades to dig them out of sand, pickaxes to remove rubble from the roads, chains in case of snow (unlikely on a trip from New York to Mexico, but it was best to cover every eventuality). Blotto didn't tell Corky to pack any guns or other weapons.

He was confident his cricket bat would provide adequate protection.

Corky Froggett kept reminding the young master that Americans drove on the wrong side of the road . . . though that didn't affect Blotto too much, as his favourite route for driving the Lagonda was straight down the middle.

So, though their car journey took them through wide varieties of countryside and passed many sights of great interest, they didn't notice any of them.

The sea crossing, incidentally, had been uneventful. The predictable things happened. Blotto was chased round the ship by a bevy of delectable young women, in whom he had no interest at all, but who had a lot of interest in him. And Corky very quickly struck up a close friendship with one of the waitresses in the First-Class Dining Room. She had the key to a linen room near the ship's engines, to whose thrummings the pair added vibrations of their own.

Blotto spent a lot of time drinking in the First-Class Lounge with Willy 'Ruffo' Walberswick. They found the ship's cellar boasted a Bordeaux almost as acceptable as The Gren's Club Claret. This they consumed copiously and, between bottles, topped themselves up with a passable Hennessy Cognac.

Meanwhile, as old muffin-toasters from Eton will, they talked about schoolday scrapes, cricket and hunting. They even, after one particularly bibulous day, when they were both thoroughly wobbulated, talked about danger.

'For me,' said Ruffo, 'it's like a jab in the giblets with a jumping cracker. I've never been one for sniffing the squiffy powders, but my need for danger makes me the worst kind of dope fiend. It's the only time I feel all my cylinders are firing to the same fizz. So, I always have to search danger out. Don't you?'

Blotto thought for a moment, then said, 'No. I'm one of those boddoes who doesn't need to search out danger. It seems to search me out. I mean, if there were six poor thimbles sitting round a bowl of cherries, I'd be the one who pulled out the viper.'

Ruffo looked confused. 'Is there likely to be a viper in a bowl of cherries?'

'Very unlikely. That's what I'm dabbing the digit on. Danger clings on to me like the smell around a wet Labrador. In any bowl of cherries I was sampling, there *would* be a viper.'

'Ah. I read your semaphore, me old kipper. So, without fiddling round the fir trees, you're saying that danger seems to search you out?'

'That's what I did say, you pillow-eared poltroon.'

'So you did. Are you also saying that you don't like danger, that you find it a bit of a candle-snuffer?'

'No, no! I'm saying I love danger like a pike loves troutlings. But I don't have to truffle it out. It truffles me out.'

'Ah, right, Blotto. That straightens the corkscrew.' Ruffo waved his arm extravagantly. 'Waiter, could you bring us another bottle of the Hennessy?'

The two old Etonians didn't show much interest in who else was on the ship, though some of the other passengers seemed to be particularly interested in them.

Blotto always attracted attention. Given the kind of clean-cut, patrician looks which make Greek gods look a bit on the shoddy side, he exercised a magnetic attraction for young women – and older women, come to that. His desirability was only increased by the fact that he had no idea of the effect he was having. Any compliment on his looks would be met by an embarrassed blush and a

13

mumbled response of 'Don't talk such toffee!' Boddoes who'd been to English public school and played cricket tended to avoid the mushy stuff. For Blotto, the idea of woman actually finding men attractive was mildly distasteful.

Willy 'Ruffo' Walberswick, whose looks were on the grittier side of classic beauty, did not attract the same level of attention. But, given the dearth of even mildly present-able young men on the transatlantic liner, he did not go unnoticed. However, the young women attracted to him were in for a disappointment. Like most journalists, Ruffo only enjoyed encounters with women in moments of extreme jeopardy. The ideal situation in which he might turn amorous was the night before infiltrating the den of a homicidal drug-dealing gang. Nothing got him more excited about a woman than the knowledge that he would never see her again. The prospect of a relationship with any element of futurity scared him to death.

Among the doe-eyed and cow-eyed young women on the ship – and a few who contrived to be doe-eyed and cow-eyed at the same time – there was one who had a lot more about her. Eschewing mammalian comparisons, her eyes had more in common with those of the eagle or hawk . . . that is to say, if an eagle or a hawk's eyes were as brown as coffee beans and prone to peering seductively from beneath heavy, sultry lashes. Anyway, the focus those eyes turned on Blotto contained more than mere admiration for his good looks.

The name of this paragon was Isadora del Plato. Famous in her native Spain as a flamenco dancer, her international travels to perform supplied an effective smokescreen for her more private activities. She came into her own when passions were at their steamiest and politics were at their seamiest. She had been in the employ of many govern-ments. Nothing so simple as an agent or a double agent, she was a multiple agent, who had been turned more times than the new leaf of a habitual renegade. The appearance of Isadora del Plato in any situation meant first, glamour. And second, trouble.

Not, of course, that Blotto was aware of any of this when the siren approached him in the First-Class Lounge on the night of their departure from Portsmouth.

'Good evening,' she susurrated in a voice of melting Spanish chocolate. 'I believe I have the privilege of addressing The Honourable Devereux Lyminster, younger son of the late Duke of Tawcester.'

'You've pinged the partridge there,' said Blotto.

'We have met before,' she purred.

Far too well brought up to say he'd never seen her in his life, Blotto said, 'Hoopee-doopee!', an expression which he found covered most eventualities. 'Pardon my pickle,' he went on, 'but I'm afraid your name has puddled down the brain-plug. Could you give the old neurons a nudge?'

'My name,' she sibilated, 'is Isadora del Plato.'

'Good ticket. All comes back to me now,' Blotto lied.

'I am a good friend of your sister, The Honourable Honoria Lyminster,' Isadora lied in her turn.

'Oh, tickey-tockey,' said Blotto. 'Muffin-toaster of the sainted Twinks – of course! That's sprinkled back the memory dust. Spoffing good to see you again!'

'And is it true that Twinks is visiting her friend Begonia Guiteras in Mexico?'

'You're snuffling towards the right truffle there!'

'Good. And you are going to join her?'

'Pinged another partridge, Isadora.'

'Splendid. Well, please, Lord Devereux—'

'Blotto.'

'I am sorry?' The flamenco dancer looked offended. 'I have had nothing to drink all evening.'

15

'No, no. Blotto – my name-tag,' he explained. 'Boddoes call me "Blotto".'

'Ah – "Blotto". From now on, I will always call you "Blotto".'

He didn't question why she didn't know that from their earlier (fictitious) encounter. Blotto didn't actually question many things. He benefited from the serene lack of curiosity visited only on the terminally thick. In Blotto's world, if you didn't ask, everything usually worked out fine.

'And, if it doesn't curdle your cream cake, from now on I will always call you "Izzy".'

'I would be enchanted if you would,' murmured Isadora del Plato.

'Toad-in-the-hole! Izzy it is!' Blotto beamed.

'And when you are with your sister in Jalapeno, Blotto, you will be happy to tell me what goes on in the house of General Henriquez Guiteras . . . ?'

'I'll be as happy as a duck in orange,' said Blotto.

It was again not in his nature to question why she might want such information. Until he had concrete proof of their wrongdoing, it was Blotto's instinct to think the best of all people (except for solicitors, of course).

During their conversation, Isadora del Plato had drawn her chair up very close to his, so that she was virtually breathing in his ear. Blotto hadn't noticed this. It was not the kind of thing he did notice.

But, from the other side of the First-Class Lounge, the pair's proximity had not gone unobserved by a swarthy man with ferociously threatening eyebrows.

Blotto had not even noticed the watcher and, if he had, he wouldn't have recognised him. But anyone in the Spanish-speaking world would instantly have identified El Falleza, the legendary bullfighter.

They would probably also have known of the famously tempestuous relationship he shared with the flamenco dancer, Isadora del Plato. It provided endless fodder for the trashier Spanish newspapers, an endless story of on and off. And, every time, what caused it to be off was the insane jealousy of El Falleza, convinced that his inamorata was having an affair with another man. Whether or not the allegation was true, the bullfighter was notorious for the violence of his revenges on the men in question.

Though, of course, blithely unaware of the fact, Blotto had that evening made a very dangerous enemy.

Once an unwilling Izzy had been led away by her smouldering bullfighter, Blotto ordered another bottle of the Bordeaux and wondered where in the name of snitchrags Ruffo had got to. He didn't really want to commune with anyone other than his old muffin-toaster from Eton. Blotto wasn't by nature antisocial, he just reckoned he already knew plenty of people he liked and wasn't too bothered about swelling their ranks.

Not everyone, however, felt as he did. There are some who regard an ocean voyage as the perfect opportunity to make new friends. One such was a tubby man trussed into an evening suit and preceded by a cigar whose length would have challenged the nose of Pinocchio at his most mendacious.

'Hi,' he said, taking – uninvited – the seat next to Blotto. Even that monosyllable revealed that he hadn't been to the right sort of schools.

'Fair biddles,' said Blotto, reckoning this to be a response which was discouraging without being actually rude. Though not the most sensitive of souls, his patrician education had made him an expert in the judgement of such nuances.

'My name's Sydney Pollard,' the tubby man volunteered.

Awkward. To deny the reciprocal information was way beyond the barbed wire, but equally Blotto had no wish to become involved in a conversation. He struck a formal note by saying tersely, 'Devereux Lyminster.'

But what Sydney Pollard said next would have melted the reserve of Blotto if he'd been a mammoth embedded in a glacier for many millennia. 'Am I right in understanding that you are the owner of that splendid Lagonda down in the hold?'

The tubby man could only have pleased Blotto more if he had included Mephistopheles and his cricket bat in the commendation. But since Sydney Pollard did not know the young man possessed a hunter or a cricket bat, no blame could be attached to him for the omission.

'Yes,' Blotto enthused. 'Bit of a buzzbanger, isn't she?'

'Well, Devereux—'

'Blotto, please, Sydney.'

'In that case, you make it "Syd".'

Blotto beamed. 'Tickey-tockey, Syd.'

Much discussion then ensued about the merits of the vehicle in question. Sydney Pollard proved himself to be no sluggard when it came to automotive knowledge. He was familiar with the engine of the Lagonda to every last sprocket. And it was after much talk of torque between the two enthusiasts, that he broached a new subject.

'I gather,' he said, 'that you are planning to drive all the way to Mexico in the Lagonda . . . ?'

'That ticks the to-do box, yes,' Blotto agreed. It never occurred for him to question how Sydney Pollard came to know so much about him.

'Then I wonder,' said his new friend, 'whether you could help me out on something . . . ?'

'Always ready to wheel out the goodwill for a fellow Lagonda-lover.'

'Splendid. Well, Blotto, you see, I'm in beef.'

That prompted a mystified, 'Ah.'

'You know what beef is?'

Blotto agreed that he did. 'It's meat from cows. Well, and bulls.'

'Exactly. I'm into the corned variety.'

'Corned cows and bulls?'

'Yes. You know what I mean?'

'I certainly do. Poor thimbles.'

'I'm sorry?'

'Well, it can't be very comfortable for the cows and bulls having corns, can it? Must make it very hard to walk. Particularly if you start off with cloven hooves in the first place. Though I'm never quite sure how they get cloven. Does someone go around when they're little with a cleaver? If so, it makes slaughtering them for beef rather a mercy, doesn't it?'

It was Sydney Pollard's turn to look mystified. This was his first encounter with Blotto's logic.

'Corned beef. Corned beef is my business. Have you heard of corned beef?'

Blotto claimed that he hadn't. The only beef seen at Tawcester Towers came bloody and untreated from the carcass. Same when he was at Eton. Even in the military, during 'the last little dust-up in France', though Corky Froggett could have expatiated at length on the pros and cons of corned beef, Blotto, being of the officer class, had subsisted on officers' rations. Which did not include corned beef.

His current ignorance of corned beef was in fact the result of selective memory. Blotto had, some years previously, travelled to the United States with a view to being married to Mary, daughter of the meat-packing magnate, Luther P. Chapstick III. And while there, he had

19

been offered the opportunity to eat the mogul's most successful product, Chapstick's Corned Beef.

But Blotto's brain had a remarkably convenient function – a self-erasing facility. When something unpleasant threatened to invade his memory, he could forget about it completely. And, so traumatic had been his encounter with the Chapstick family, that he now had no recollection of it. All that remained of that transatlantic experience was the comforting warm glow that arose from having once again escaped matrimony. So, he genuinely believed that he had never before heard the words 'corned beef'.

'So, is it,' he asked cautiously of Sydney Pollard, 'something you eat?'

'Yes. Treated with salts, sealed into cans, lasts forever.'

'Ah,' said Blotto, intrigued by this moment of insight into how the other ninety-nine-point-nine per cent live.

'So, you're in trade, are you?' he asked. Trade was another thing of which his upbringing had rendered him totally ignorant.

'Yes,' said Sydney Pollard. 'In trade and proud of it.'

Blotto laughed. Always liked a boddo with a sense of humour.

'And, as a man of international commerce,' the tubby man pressed on, 'I am very concerned about the fate of the less fortunate people in the world.'

Blotto couldn't make head or tail of that assertion. He didn't know much about the world of business, but he did know that success in that world was always based on the exploitation of 'the less fortunate people in the world'. That was how the Lyminsters and families like them had built the huge fortunes they had spent so many generations squandering.

'Anyway,' Sydney Pollard went on, 'my current mission is to supply – free and gratis – tins of corned beef to the starving children of Mexico.'

'Beezer wheeze!' said Blotto.

'And I was wondering, since you're going to be driving down there, whether you could see your way to transporting some of the corned beef supplies there in your Lagonda?'

'For the starving children of Mexico?'

'Exactly!'

'Sounds like a bingbopper of an idea to me!' said Blotto.

'And I was thinking, to avoid unnecessary scrutiny from officious border officials, you could hide the corned beef in the secret compartment that is installed under the Lagonda's chassis.'

'Another buzzbanger!' Blotto enthused.

'So, you'll do it?'

'Will I do it? Do the French like cheese? Of course I'll do it,' said Blotto.

Being of a trusting nature, he didn't bother to ask any follow-up questions. Like for instance, how Sydney Pollard knew about the secret compartment which had been fitted to the Lagonda by the Mafia during an earlier trip across the Pond. And, come to that, why, given that corned beef was one of the major exports of the area, Sydney Pollard wanted to get the stuff *into* Mexico.

Pleased to have achieved the agreement he was after, the meat magnate soon drifted out of the First-Class Lounge.

Then, finally, Willy 'Ruffo' Walberswick appeared, signalling the start of the epic drinking sessions which would occupy him and Blotto for the rest of the voyage.

Meanwhile, down in the liner's hold, following the instructions of Sydney Pollard, a number of heavy wooden crates were transferred from a lorry to the secret compartment of the Lagonda. On the side of each crate was

21

stamped the company slogan: 'Pollard's Corned Beef – That's the Stuff to Give the Troops!'

Corky Froggett, preoccupied with his First-Class Dining Room waitress, was unaware that the transfer had taken place.

Twinks in Mexico

While Blotto braved the Atlantic Ocean and the highways of the USA, his sister was enjoying life in Mexico with her friend Begonia Guiteras. Though not on the same intellectual level as Twinks – no one except Professor Erasmus Holofernes actually was, and it was a close call with him – the girl proved an amiable companion. The pair enjoyed riding over the dusty Mexican terrain, so different from the lazy green undulations of Tawcestershire. (Twinks, unlike her brother, *did* notice the scenery around her.) And their evenings were spent at a surprising variety of dinners and balls, indulgences of the wealthy in Jalapeno Province. (Though Willy 'Ruffo' Walberswick had singled out the area as the scene of a forthcoming 'international incident', the prospect had had no effect on the local social life.)

Wherever the two girls went, they made a vivid impression. Each beautiful in her own right, their appearance together supplied an image to satisfy every masculine fantasy. Begonia was a classic Hispanic archetype, with a generous figure, lustrous black hair, full lips, and teeth which cried out to bite on a tango rose.

Twinks, by contrast, was a symphony in translucence. Her skin had often been compared to alabaster, usually by people who had no idea what alabaster was. (Blotto thought it was a vegetable.) Her cheeks were touched with a rose-petal blush. Her hair was described as being like spun gold or spun silver, usually by people who'd never tried spinning either. Her eyes were pools of azure mystery, in which many men had lost their footing and drowned. And her figure was as deliciously minimal as Begonia's was voluptuous. So far as male desire was concerned, the two of them covered all the bases.

Unlike her brother, who had no knowledge of, or interest in, politics, Twinks was well aware of the chaotic post-revolutionary situation in Mexico. Before her trip to Jalapeno, she had consulted Professor Erasmus Holofernes, who knew everything about everything political, and he had given her an up-to-date briefing on the state of the nation.

So, unseduced by the surface calm, Twinks was aware of the implications of everything she witnessed out there. Though, of course, no one would have guessed it from her demeanour. She and Begonia, who was also highly intelligent, played up to the image of pleasure-seeking socialites, who possibly shared a single braincell between them. In the male-dominated upper-class circles of Mexico, this pose went down very well. In that country, many things were expected of women, but thinking was not among them.

Twinks charmed and smiled and behaved exactly as if the space between her ears was as unoccupied as that between Blotto's.

Though that was how she presented herself to Mexican society, she ensured that Professor Hector Troon-Wheatley

24

saw a very different woman, an intellectual equal with a deep understanding of Aztec civilisation.

The dig he was organising in Jalapeno was in some natural caves, set high in a mountainous area and known locally as the 'Attatotalloss Caves', where there was evidence of an early civilisation. Troon-Wheatley, in the face of considerable academic opposition, was determined to prove that those people were the direct ancestors of the Aztecs. This went against the accepted wisdom that the Aztecs were hunter/gatherers who migrated from the north to central Mexico.

It went without saying that Twinks had read up enough about the subject to have an informed opinion. And, on the basis of the evidence she had accumulated, she supported Troon-Wheatley's theory.

There was also a local legend, much pooh-poohed by serious archaeologists, that somewhere in that area of Jalapeno there lay a hoard of gold, stolen from the Aztecs by the sixteenth-century Conquistadors, stashed away in a secret hiding place for collection later. Local conflicts and an outbreak of plague at the time had prevented the loot ever being reclaimed. Over the centuries, many treasure hunters had tried to track down these mythical riches, but without success.

It hardly needs saying that Professor Hector Troon-Wheatley had no interest in this fabled Conquistadors' gold. His private income had inoculated him against acquisitiveness. He worshipped knowledge rather than filthy lucre. And the Conquistadors were far too recent a civilisation to hold any interest for him as an archaeologist.

Though he and Twinks had corresponded, the Professor was already out in Mexico when Professor Erasmus Holofernes's idea of her helping him came up, so they hadn't met until her arrival in Jalapeno. And it is fair to say that Twinks was not what Troon-Wheatley had been expecting. For a start, there was the issue of gender. Holofernes's letters had referred to the recommended helper merely as 'Twinks', and the archaeologist had made the reasonable assumption that this was the mildly unusual nickname by which this fellow academic was known in Oxford. So, the appearance of an indisputably female newcomer at the excavation was his first surprise.

Troon-Wheatley had always been far too obsessed with his studies to notice women, and most of the ones he met on digs might as well have been men, anyway. Both genders dressed in khaki army-style shirts, riding breeches and stout boots. Permanent layers of dust made them even less distinguishable. And conversation about things other than bone fragments and shards of pottery was discouraged.

So, when Twinks, dressed in a practical (but flattering) beige suit cut on military lines, shimmered out of the heat haze towards him at the cave entrance, Professor Hector Troon-Wheatley found himself the victim of feelings he had never felt before.

It should be pointed out at this point that the Professor suffered from the same handicap, born of public-school education, as Twinks's brother. He never thought about his looks, and it would never have occurred to him that he might be attractive to a woman – or indeed that anyone of his gender could be attractive to a woman.

Which was rather sad, perhaps, because he was an extraordinarily good-looking man, who could have given Blotto a run in the Greek God steeplechase. Long exposure to sunlight had turned his skin the colour of a croissant and produced the most endearing of wrinkles around his black eyes. Endless digging and lifting had tuned his body to a symphony of muscle. His hair and beard, both worn long from the extended unavailability of a barber, were curly and black, with glints of sparkle from the sand captured in them. And his white teeth gleamed when his jaw dropped at the sight of his new assistant.

'And are you really "Twinks"?'

'You've potted the black there. But, if you want my more formal name-tag, it's "Lady Honoria Lyminster".'

'Lady Honoria Lyminster, eh?'

'I'm only called that, though, by poshos or people the wrong side of the green baize door. To all my chumbos, I'm Twinks. And, either I've pongled a long way after a dead duck, or you're Professor Hector Troon-Wheatley.'

'I am.'

'And what do people call you?'

He looked puzzled and replied, 'Professor Hector Troon-Wheatley.'

'Splendissimo!' said Twinks. 'I will call you "Heckie".'

'Oh.' The Professor didn't look entirely happy with that news. But he did look extremely happy about Twinks's arrival.

When her conversation proved to be as informed about the Aztecs as her letters had been, he seemed to be transported to a new and rarefied land. Was it possible that he could become interested in something less than five centuries old?

'So,' said Twinks, 'larksissimo to see you, Heckie. Can't wait to see how the spoffing excavation's going.'

'Bit of a rum baba, I'm afraid,' the Professor said. 'I was ready to start the whole shooting match, convinced I was close to the entrance to the lower level of caves. And I'd got a nifty squad of local helpers. Just peons, really, don't speak any English, don't know one end of a fossil from the other, but cheery souls, willing to learn. So, the dig was all diggety and I could get down to some serious specimen-sifting . . . and then, suddenly, this morning, the whole caravan packed their tents and went back to their villages. With no intention of working for me again.'

He gestured helplessly to a section of the cave wall, where a collection of spades, pickaxes, crowbars, brushes and buckets were stacked.

'Why?' asked Twinks. 'Is it because they're going to winch up their weapons and join the war?'

'What war?' asked Troon-Wheatley.

'Oh, don't don your worry-boots about that,' said Twinks. Everyone knew that General Henriquez Guiteras's declaration of independence for Jalapeno was bound to lead to armed conflict, but the Professor didn't need to concern himself with such details. 'So, why have they bundled up their bedrolls and biffed off?'

'The word has spread among the numbnoddies that the Attatotalloss Caves are cursed.'

'Cursed? That's a tough rusk to chew.'

'It is indeed, but that's what the Mexican workers are saying. Their gangmaster, a man called Refritos, insists that his men cannot work here any longer.'

'But who's put the hoofing hex on them?'

'Refritos says that, if I dig further into the caves, I will cause sacrilege to the sacred Aztec burial grounds and unleash the dreaded Curse of Attatotalloss!'

'And what's that when it's got its spats on?'

'Local legend. Old wives' tale, more likely. The caves are supposed to be guarded by the spirit of Attatotalloss, who was some Aztec God King. If anyone invades his territory, his ghost is rumoured to confront them.'

'And what does this ghastible ghost look like?'

'Oh, sort of man-shaped, a black body smeared with ancient mud. And a black headdress with a kind of beak-like protuberance at the front. All superstitious nonsense, as I say. But some of the peons still believe it.'

'So, does the Ghost of Attatotalloss coffinate the intruders – or what?'

'Oh yes. According to the legend, anyone who sets eyes on him will die in agony within the week.'

'And is there any evidence of this ever having happened, Heckie?'

'For goodness' sake, Twinks! Of course there isn't. It's just a folk tale. Wouldn't stand up to a second of scientific scrutiny.'

'But it is rather grandissimo!' said Twinks, for whom the prospect of the caves being haunted just added another level of excitement.

Life at the Guiteras Ranch was a hymn to hedonism. The General surrounded himself with hangers-on who indulged cheerfully in his lavish hospitality. The casual observer would have assumed that the only aim of those present was the pursuit of pleasure.

Twinks, of course, was far from a casual observer. Sensitive to the subtlest of nuances in every situation, she was aware of the tensions beneath the playful image of the ranch. Steeped in the recent history of Mexico, the civil war which had taken up most of the twentieth century's second decade and the more recent take-over of power by the Partido Nacional Revolucionario, Twinks understood the fragility of the new regime and the risks that General Henriquez Guiteras was taking by declaring the independence of Jalapeno. As yet, no military reprisals had been taken against him, but Twinks knew it was only a matter of time till government forces came to crush the uprising.

The General himself betrayed no signs of anxiety. He knew that the troops he had in the barracks on the edge of the Guiteras Ranch were superior in numbers and training to the ragtag army being slowly assembled by the Partido Nacional Revolucionario. So, he awaited the forthcoming conflict with relaxed confidence and the appearance of indolence.

When he wasn't careering round his realm on horseback with a posse of desperados, the General was seated at a table on a vine-shaded terrace, eating steaks bigger than the plates they were served on, quaffing tequila and smoking cigars the size of cucumbers. He wore a white military uniform to which he kept adding a variety of tassels, gold braid and sashes. And all the while he kept up a flow of boasting about his prowess in the battlefield and the bedroom. His acolytes endorsed his extravagant claims and laughed sycophantically at his jokes.

The most assiduous of the General's toadies was called Colonel Pedro Jiminez. He wore black moustaches and big hats and left no swash unbuckled (and in fact no buckle unswashed). He spoke excellent English, and he definitely knew his place in the Guiteras Ranch hierarchy. When the boss was there, he reacted admiringly to his braggadocio. But when the General was off the scene, Jiminez was not backward in blowing his own trumpet.

He believed himself to be fatally attractive to women. Though wary around Begonia – the General did not take kindly to men expressing carnal interest in his daughter, he had his own plans for her – Jiminez suffered from no such inhibition when it came to Twinks. Living his entire life in Mexico and therefore unused to such visions of pale translucence, he was instantly captivated. Having grown up having all his wishes granted by an indulgent mother and every other woman he encountered, it did not occur to him that Twinks might not be as besotted as he was with Colonel Pedro Jiminez.

When first introduced to her, he announced in heavily accented English, 'You will marry me, Lady Honoria.'

'Not in a year of Decembers,' said Twinks with glacial charm.

'I am sorry. You do not understand. I said that you will marry me.'

'And I said – in case you did not understand my idiom – that is something I will not do till hell is converted to an ice-rink.'

'Still, you do not understand. Perhaps you do not realise who I am.'

'I have been told your spoffing name. I know you to be Colonel Pedro Jiminez, a military man with some meaningless Mexican rank and self-esteem the size of a barrage balloon.'

'You have been misinformed.'

'I haven't been informed, let alone *mis*informed. I had never even heard your name-tag until we were introduced a matter of moments ago.'

He looked shocked. 'You mean that the great country of Britain does not resound with praise for the valorous deeds of Colonel Pedro Jiminez?'

Twinks adopted her mother the Dowager Duchess's North-Face-of-the-Eiger look. 'I can assure you that, back in the cradle of civilisation, no one knows a blind bezonger about you. The average ant is more highly esteemed in polite society than Colonel Pedro Jiminez.'

He chuckled heartily. 'Do not worry, Lady Honoria Lyminster. When we are married, you will understand what a prince among men you have been fortunate enough to entrap with your feminine wiles.'

Twinks's exquisite jaw set firm. Colonel Pedro Jiminez was an irritant and a challenge. But only a minor challenge, nothing to worry her. She had spent much of her life convincing men to take no for an answer. She was an international expert at the craft.

The main house on the Guiteras Ranch was built on palatial scale around an area of cooling courtyards. The predominant colour was terra-cotta and the courtyards were linked by a proliferation of black wrought-iron gates.

Begonia and Twinks's bedrooms shared a balcony and, at the end of the day after their late dinner, when the men lingered over their tequila, cigars and boasting, the two young women would sit out there. It would be the first time since dawn that the air felt even mildly cool.

They would be joined by Begonia's menagerie. From an early age, the girl had been devoted to animals. The courtyards of the Guiteras Ranch were well equipped with kennels and hutches for her various pets. Dogs, cats, white rabbits and guinea pigs abounded. The dogs and cats, having spent their days sprawled out unmoving in the shade, came alive with the onset of evening, and liked to join the two girls on the balcony.

Their viewpoint looked out through the dusk, across verdant plains to the distant, rippling outlines of the mountains. Such moments could have been designed for the sharing of secrets, and it was an opportunity of which Twinks and Begonia took full advantage.

'That Colonel Pedro Jiminez,' Twinks confided to her friend, 'thinks he's the panda's panties, doesn't he?'

Begonia agreed. 'In Mexico all men are brought up to believe they are gods.'

'Then that puffed-up pouncepot does a great recruiting job for atheism.'

'But women,' said Begonia sadly, 'are always bound to be inferior to men. That is the role we are born to play.'

'What a load of plipping plankton!' said Twinks. 'Do you really believe that diddle-doddle?'

'It is what my parents have brought me up to believe.'

'Then your parents have very definitely got the wrong end of the sink plunger. Men are full of puff and piffle, but who actually makes things happen?'

'My father always says men make things happen.'

'Then he's a total numbnoddy. In every situation, it's women who sport the spats.' Growing up in Tawcester Towers, witnessing how the Dowager Duchess dominated all the masculine limp-rags on the scene, had made it very clear to Twinks where the true power lay. And to find someone of her own gender who didn't appreciate that ancient truth always upset her.

'What you've got to do, Begonia,' she went on, 'is neutralise the negativity in that noddle of yours. Men moan that they don't know what women want, but women themselves know. And it's our spoffing duty, as women, to get what we want! So don't ever let a man put hampertraps in your path, Begonia.'

'But my father is such a strong man.' Begonia was devoutly repeating a formula that she had heard every day of her childhood. 'Nobody has ever argued with General Henriquez Guiteras.'

'Then it's about time his peepers were deblinkered. You implied he had some fumacious plans for you . . . ?'

'Only who I marry.'

'"Only"? Has the blunderthug got some grisly groom lined up for you?'

'He has told me that I have to marry one of his Colonels.'

'Not Colonel Pedro Jiminez?'

'No. Another. Colonel Alfredo Maldonado. An older man. A man my father's age.'

'The slugbucket!'

'You can see him down there.' Begonia pointed. Twinks saw, sitting at a table in the courtyard below, lit by candle-light, two men in military uniforms. One she recognised as Begonia's father. But the other . . . If he was the same age as General Henriquez Guiteras, then he had misused his youth shockingly. He looked to be more of an age to be Begonia's grandfather.

'Rats in a sandwich!' said Twinks. 'I hope they've already measured him for his coffin.'

'He's more robust than he appears. He keeps telling me what a great lover he is.'

'Yuk! That's a real slug in the shower. Presumably, you don't have any tender feelings for this Colonel Alfredo Maldonado?'

'He repels me.'

'I'm not surprised. Even his own mother would avert her eyes. Anyway, we must change your father's running order. You can't have this geriatric gigolo stuck on you like an unwanted corn plaster!'

'But how can I stop it happening?' asked a despairing Begonia. 'It is my father's wish.'

'Your father must learn that his wish is way the wrong side of the running rail.' Twinks was distracted by another thought. 'Tell me, Begonia,' she breathed, 'is there another boddo, a young, tasty slice of redcurrant cheese-cake, who you *do* love?'

Tears glistened in Begonia's black-brown eyes, as she murmured, 'Yes. Yes, there is. He is a man of enormous charm and considerable academic achievements. For example, as well as his native Spanish, he speaks perfect English, French and Italian.'

'Grandissimo!' said Twinks.

'Not so grandissimo,' said Begonia. 'Because of all the men I could have chosen to love, none is less suitable, from the point of view of my father, than Carlos Contreras.'

'Why, what has the poor thimble done to curdle your father's cream?'

'It is not so much what he has done, it is who he is.'

'Sorry? Not reading your semaphore.'

'Carlos is the son of General Ignacio Contreras,' Begonia announced dramatically.

'Ah. And who's he when he's got his spats on?'

'General Ignacio Contreras is the governor of Jalapeno Province, appointed by the Partido Nacional Revolucionario.'

'The boddoes who claim to pull the puppet strings all over Mexico?'

'Exactly. The central power which my father has challenged by declaring the independence of Jalapeno Province.'

'Great spangled spiders!' murmured Twinks, getting caught up in the excitement of the situation. 'And where are the General and Carlos now? Back at the Partido Nacional Revolucionario headquarters, rustling up an army to put your father's Jack back in its Box?'

'No, my father's men caught them before they could escape. Carlos and the General are currently in Jalapeno City Jail, facing charges of insurrection.'

'But that's a bit banana-shaped. If any stencher has been doing any insurrecting, then it's your Pater, not General Ignacio Contreras.'

'Exactly, Twinks. But my father has a nasty habit of making up laws to suit his convenience. And he's made a law, specially designed to set up the two Contrerases on charges of insurrection.'

'The four-faced filcher!' said Twinks before she could stop herself. 'Oh, sorry, plumped for the wrong plum there. Shouldn't mud-smudge your Pater while I'm on camomile lawns enjoying his hospitality.'

'Don't worry about that,' said Begonia. 'I have no illusions about my father's character. Basically, he's a blunderthug.'

'Glad those words came out of your toothtrap rather than mine, Beggers.'

'I have spent too much of my life making excuses for his behaviour. All my life, he's been feeding me the wrong spaghetti. It is time for me to admit that I am the daughter of a man who wouldn't recognise a moral if it bit him on the shin.'

'Fair biddles, chumbo,' said Twinks. Then she continued, with some *délicatesse*, 'Presumably, when it comes to these laws your Pater gets such a zizzy tingle from inventing . . .'

'What?'

'. . . they come with penalties attached. A whole sequence of murdy knuckleraps for the guilty, eh?'

'Yes, they do.' The air seemed constricted in Begonia's throat. 'My father enjoys devising punishments.'

'So, what's the time tariff for insurrection?'

With difficulty, Begonia replied, 'Death by firing squad.'

'Great galumphing goatherds!' said Twinks. In her azure eyes glowed the sparkle that the prospect of adventure always kindled there.

4

El Chipito

Blotto was a bit miffed when he and Corky were asked to produce their passports at the Mexican border. He had been brought up with the view that, if you'd been born into an aristocratic family and gone to Eton, you should be allowed to pass unimpeded wherever you wanted to go. All doors were permanently open to you. That was certainly how things worked back in England.

But the Mexican border officials seemed never to have heard of Tawcester Towers. They were, in fact, positively hostile, suspicious as to what business a scion of the Lyminster line might have in their country. And when Blotto said he was coming to join up with Twinks, they seemed – remarkably – not to have heard of her either. He had to remind himself that he was perhaps in a country whose educational standards did not match up to those of Eton.

Then something very rare happened. A thought struck Blotto. And he realised, of course, that it wasn't him engendering suspicion in the Mexican border guards. It was Corky Froggett. Blotto would never draw attention to it, but the fact remained that Corky was, socially, only one step up from the serfs who had uncomplainingly ministered to the Lyminsters' every need during the wonderful period of the feudal system. The Mexican border guards, little more than peasants or peons themselves, recognised one of their own, and treated him accordingly.

If the chauffeur hadn't been with him, Blotto felt sure he'd have had a much easier border experience. The guards wouldn't have submitted the Lagonda to such a thorough search, for one thing. Nor would they have handled Blotto's cricket bat with such overt suspicion, he felt sure. Its owner's customary equanimity had been threatened at that moment. Watching the heavily moustachioed guards manhandling the precious willow had raised every hackle Blotto had. And his attempts to explain to them what the mysterious object was for fell on deaf ears. They did not respond with any level of understanding to his mimes of a cover drive and a reverse sweep.

Indeed, they seemed convinced that the cricket bat was some kind of weapon. There was even a suggestion of their confiscating it. Fortunately, that didn't happen. Which was just as well. Blotto's response to such sacrilege would have enabled Willy 'Ruffo' Walberswick to add another to his list of 'international incidents'.

When, finally, they were allowed to leave the border post on the dusty road south, Blotto, who was driving the Lagonda, observed to Corky, 'Well, we pinged the partridge with what we were gabbing about back at the old T Towers, didn't we?'

'I'm sorry? To what are you referring, milord?'

'Back on home hay, we raised the quezzie as to whether the Mexicans played cricket.'

'Ah yes. On the same page, milord.'

'And I think we can now answer it with a resounding "Not on your nuthatch!"'

'We certainly can, milord.'

'Still, no icing off my birthday cake. Teaching the Mexicans how to address willow to leather will be absolutely the lark's larynx.'

'Spot on, milord.'

'Did you have a little frissonette, Corky, when the guards were searching the Lag?'

'No, milord. I felt confident they would find nothing.' Because, so far as Corky was concerned, there was nothing to find. He did not know about the Lagonda's clandestine cargo.

'Me too,' Blotto agreed. 'Spoffing good job those Mafia numbnoddies did, didn't they?'

'An excellent job, milord.'

They referred to a time, once again on the wrong side of the Atlantic, when Blotto had got involved in the affairs of the Cosa Nostra who, for purposes of their own, affixed beneath the chassis of the Lagonda a compartment big enough to accommodate two bodies . . . or any other goods which needed surreptitious transportation. On various occasions, the question had arisen as to whether the compartment should be removed from the Lagonda, but the decision had always been to keep it in place.

Which was very convenient, given that now the space was filled with crates on whose sides was stencilled: 'Pollard's Corned Beef – That's the Stuff to Give the Troops!' A charitable gift of corned beef tins for the starving children of Mexico.

Or so Blotto believed.

Willy 'Ruffo' Walberswick had continued from New York to the Mexican port of Veracruz by ship, and thereafter made his way by a series of taxis, hired cars, ox-carts and horses to Jalapeno Province. Fortunately, he spoke extremely good Spanish, which he needed to out there.

Ruffo was in his element. Everywhere he looked, he faced danger. He could trust no one. Every local he dealt with – every driver, every hotel keeper, every fellow traveller – might have a reason to kill him. This was the life he relished. The only minor disappointment was that he hadn't yet encountered a woman with whom he could share a night of passion before facing the next death-defying challenge.

Of course, as he went on his way, Ruffo was continuing his work as a journalist, questioning everyone he met about the political situation in Mexico and, in particular, the reaction of the central government to Jalapeno's recent declaration of independence. Primitive communication systems meant he wouldn't be able to file his copy back to the London news desk until he was back at Veracruz on his return trip. But he was determined that, by then, he would have built up a dossier which covered every aspect of the conflict. Pleasing images of his receiving awards for his reporting lurked at the back of his mind.

On his journey from the port, he managed to infiltrate the spy networks of both sides and had to distinguish the lies told by the Partido Nacional Revolucionario spies from those told by General Henriquez Guiteras's spies. Ruffo felt he was getting near the truth when he reached the boundary of Jalapeno Province and had a clear run to the province's main city which, rather conveniently, was called 'Jalapeno City'.

There he was introduced, through a network of dubious contacts, to a man called El Chipito. They met in a cellar bar, shadowy, but not too shadowy for Ruffo to see that all of the customers were armed to the teeth. When he was sat down opposite El Chipito, he was aware of a general shifting as a security ring of hostile human beings was formed around their table.

The candlelight that flickered across El Chipito's face added other lines to the one long diagonal scar that stretched down from eyebrow to jawline.

'So,' asked the desperado in surprisingly good English, 'what do you want with El Chipito?'

Ruffo had done his research. 'First,' he said, 'I would like to say that I am honoured to meet a man whose achievements have reached such legendary status.'

The look that came after his nod indicated that El Chipito wanted more flattery.

'I have followed your military career with great interest,' Ruffo continued. 'You have fought in many wars, and you have a unique record of having always ended up on the winning side . . . .'

Another gratified nod.

'. . . even if that is not the side on which you started the conflict.'

It was a calculated risk, which triggered a sharp intake of breath from the encircling thugs, as they waited to see how their boss would react. But, after a long moment, El Chipito smiled.

'You have analysed my career very well,' he said. 'The first rule of war is to be on the winning side. And, usually, the winning side is the one that can pay you most. This has been the principle that has guided the career of El Chipito.'

'To very good effect,' said Ruffo. 'So, tell me, which will be the winning side in the battle for Jalapeno?'

A smile cut across the scarred face. 'Obviously, as you have so clearly worked out, the side that I am on.'

'Which is?'

'I am starting on the side of the Mexican government. The Partido Nacional Revolucionario have paid me to get together an army to crush the renegade General Henriquez Guiteras.'

'They have paid you a lot, I am sure.'

'We reached a very satisfactory arrangement, yes. I have received half of the money – in gold, of course. When I have put down the uprising, I receive the other half.'

'Again in gold?'

'Of course. And when I receive the second half, I also get a bonus, a special reward.'

'Ah. And what is that?'

'My special reward . . .' An evil grin once again bisected the scar. '. . . will be General Henriquez Guiteras's daughter, Begonia.'

It was a thoughtful Twinks who rode out the next morning from the Guiteras Ranch to the site of Professor Hector Troon-Wheatley's excavations. Though not allying herself with the rather déclassé activities of the Suffragette Movement, she was a great believer in women's freedom. Having witnessed throughout her childhood the potency of the Dowager Duchess of Tawcester, she knew that there was nothing a man could do that couldn't be better achieved by one of her own gender. And the plight that Begonia Guiteras had described to her the previous evening had distressed her considerably.

To have the only man she loved imprisoned by her father and facing death by firing squad . . . well, that was far from being the panda's panties. Then to be forced into marriage to an elderly and hideous Colonel whom she loathed . . . poor Beggers. Of course, Twinks didn't know about the additional threat to Begonia from El Chipito. But she was determined somehow to save her friend from the fate that was being lined up for her.

When Twinks dismounted at the mouth of the cave, Professor Hector Troon-Wheatley was surprised to see her. 'I didn't think you'd come.'

'Why, in the name of strawberries, not?'

'Because I told you about the Curse of Attatotalloss.'

'I think stories of ancient curses are a load of absolute guff, made up by slugbuckets with an eye to the main stingo. My bro Blotto and I once got the wrong end of the sink plunger with something called "The Curse of Pharaoh Sinus Nefertop". Turned out to be some murdy sneakery rustled up by a bad tomato who was as devious as a three-dollar note. He was just trying to stitch us up like a pair of moccasins and stop our investigation. I'm sure the same thing's happened with this fumacious Curse of Attatotalloss. The whole set-up's as unconvincing as a headwaiter's toupee.'

'You mean you will continue to help me with my excavations?' he asked hopefully.

'That's why I pongled all the way over here from the Land of the Golden Lions. If you don't want my help, then the whole voyagette has been rather a waste of gingerbread.'

'Oh, but I do want your help,' Troon-Wheatley assured her.

'Larksissimo, Heckie,' said Twinks. 'Then no more fiddling round the fir trees. Let's start ticking off the to-dos.' She rolled up the sleeves of her beige military jacket, revealing slender pale arms which stirred the Professor strangely.

Trying to keep his eyes off them, he said: 'Well, the first thing that needs doing is to find the entrance to the lower caves. I'm convinced they exist. There are some old Aztec carvings found at this level which suggest they do exist. But so far, I haven't been able to find anything that looks like an opening.'

'Maybe, if I pass my peepers over the carvings, I'll spot something you missed.'

43

Professor Hector Troon-Wheatley was proud enough of his reputation to assert that he was unlikely to have missed anything. He was, after all, the world's most distinguished expert on Aztec carving.

'Oh yes, I'm sure you're a whale among whales on the subject. But you never know, a fresh pair of pryers might come up with the silverware.'

The Professor's expression showed that he was not convinced.

'Are you of the view,' asked Twinks coolly, 'that the tradition of Aztec stone carving started with the basalt workshops developed by the Olmec peoples of the Gulf Coast in the second millennium B.C., or are you snuffling towards the truffle of the whole clangdumble having begun earlier?'

Many observers would have recorded the phenomenon of Troon-Wheatley's jaw literally dropping, but Twinks was so used to the depth of her knowledge having that effect on people that she didn't notice.

With a new respect in his voice, the Professor replied, 'I am of the latter opinion. I think the Olmecs derived from the Mokaya or Mixe-Zoque cultures, and it is with them that the stone-carving tradition developed.'

'Give that pony a rosette!' said Twinks. 'We're on the same bus. So, Heckie, will you show me the carving?'

'Of course,' he said, leading her out of the sunlight into the recesses of the cave. 'I would appreciate the opinion of someone so versed in Olmec culture.'

'Jollissimo!' said Twinks.

But their immediate exploration was delayed by the sound of a car engine approaching. Professor Hector Troon-Wheatley reached for the Accrington-Murphy revolver he kept in a holster on his belt. The people who drove cars in Jalapeno Province tended not to be the most trustworthy individuals. In fact, frequently the people who drove the cars had stolen them from the trustworthy people who owned them.

Twinks raised a delicate hand to shield her eyes as they re-emerged into the sunlight.

'Oh, triple jollissimo!' she cried, as she recognised, through its cloud of dust, the outline of a familiar Lagonda. 'It's Blotters!'

The magnificent vehicle came to rest outside the cave entrance. Though Corky Froggett still cleaned each individual square inch of the bodywork every morning, it took a matter of moments, on the roads of Mexico, for the gleaming blue paint to be once again covered in dust. Now the Lagonda looked like some triumph of Parisian patisserie, dusted with icing sugar. The driver and passenger were similarly decorated.

Blotto leapt from the driving seat in one easy movement, which did not involve opening the door. On the other side, Corky Froggett disembarked more sedately.

'Now we're rolling on camomile lawns!' cried Twinks. 'How're your fetlocks foozling, Blotto me old buttoned boot?'

'Fetlocks in fizzling form!' he assured her. 'And how're your daisy chains dingling, Twinks me old football-lacer?'

'My daisy chains are linking like a Cartier necklace,' said Twinks. 'Beezer to clap the old peepers on you, Blotters!'

'My peepers reckon it's the lark's larynx to see you, Twinkers!' said Blotto.

Professor Hector Troon-Wheatley looked on in open-mouthed amazement. He was brilliant at languages. He had pieced together enough of the local dialect to understand every word spoken by his Mexican workers But the language of these two of his own compatriots had him totally baffled.

Blotto and Twinks stood looking at each other in total delight. An observer who did not know the *mores* of the British aristocracy might have thought it strange that they didn't fall into each other's arms. But people of their breeding didn't do hugging . . . or any other physical contact, actually.

5

Pollard's Plotting

There was only one hotel in Jalapeno City, called the Cactus Flower. The paintwork on its once-splendid wooden façade was sun-bleached and cracking. There had been few guests during the decade-long Mexican Revolution and the place had become run down. Now it was used only by occasional oil prospectors and the local 'ladies of the night'.

So, it was unusual that, at the time of Blotto and Corky Froggett's arrival in the country, there were three guests staying at the hotel who weren't Mexican nationals.

Sydney Pollard spent most of his time in the bar, chain-smoking his long cigars and drinking the rough, so-called brandy. He also listened to the talk of the locals, many of whom were in the employ of Colonel Henriquez Guiteras. From frequent visits to the country, Pollard's Mexican Spanish was excellent. But he looked so obviously foreign that it would never have occurred to the bar's regulars that he understood what they were saying. Accordingly, they put no curbs on their conversation, and he found out a great deal about the current state of Mexican politics.

He was particularly interested in the state of play between Colonel Henriquez Guiteras and the central

Mexican government, the Partido Nacional Revolucionario, represented by El Chipito. He knew that conflict between the two was inevitable and wanted to know which side was likely to come out the victor. Just like El Chipito, Sydney Pollard had a very long track record in ending up on the winning side in conflicts (whichever side he might have started out on).

As ever, Sydney Pollard's eye was firmly fixed on the main chance.

Amongst the varied information he received from eavesdropping on the hotel bar's regulars were two pieces of news that he had been waiting for. The first was that the local workers had stopped working at Professor Hector Troon-Wheatley's dig, supposedly frightened off by the Curse of Attatotalloss.

And the second was that The Honourable Devereux Lyminster, a.k.a. Blotto, had arrived at the Guiteras Ranch.

The two other non-Mexican guests in the hotel spent most of their time upstairs in their bedrooms. Occasionally in the same bedroom, more often in separate ones.

Isadora del Plato spent the hour between nine and ten every morning doing her flamenco practice. For this she used her portable gramophone. The beat of the music and the pounding of her heavily shod feet shuddered through the hotel's ancient wooden structure. But nobody complained about the noise. Nobody ever complained about anything done by Isadora del Plato.

The rest of her time was spent by her open window, through which pigeons kept arriving and departing. From the legs of the arrivals, she removed small metal cylinders containing rolled-up messages in tiny spidery writing. And no pigeon was allowed to depart before she had written a reply (in tiny spidery writing) and reattached the cylinder to its leg.

The information Isadora received from her pigeons was mostly related to her work as a multiple agent. Like Willy 'Ruffo' Walberswick, though from different motives, she was in Jalapeno City in anticipation of the next 'international incident'. She knew the exact number of troops General Henriquez Guiteras was keeping in readiness in their barracks adjacent to the Guiteras Ranch. She knew that, though they had been recruited – or press-ganged into service – as humble peons, the General had trained them to be highly dangerous and efficient fighting men.

Isadora also knew the numbers of pro-Partido Nacional Revolucionario troops massing on the Jalapeno borders under the command of El Chipito. She knew that they had not yet massed in sufficient numbers to risk initiating the inevitable onslaught against General Henriquez Guiteras's forces. But, every hour, her pigeons brought her updated news of the military situation. This she assessed shrewdly, working out when the conflict would erupt and, more importantly, which side would come out on top.

Amongst Isadora del Plato's avian helpers, there was one less likely bird than a pigeon. A toucan. Toucans are not renowned for their homing skills and there are no records of their being used to carry messages in warfare. But this particular toucan had been brought up from a hatchling by Isadora and had been trained, from then on, to carry messages. Wildlife experts might claim that such a feat was impossible, that it went against nature, that no toucan could ever be an efficient messenger. But such experts had not come up against the iron will of Isadora del Plato. When she told a creature to do something, the creature – be it human or animal or avian – did exactly what she told it to do.

49

While the flamenco dancer kept up her secret corres-pondence, in the adjacent bedroom, the bullfighter lay on a couch and brooded. Though occasionally granted access to Isadora's room (and the delights it offered), El Falleza spent every moment when she wasn't in his sight seething with jealousy. His threatening eyebrows knitted together in anguish. Though Isadora's pigeon post concerned much more weighty matters, El Falleza was convinced that every missive was communication with another lover.

The numbers of these kept growing in his fevered mind and he devised ever more grotesque murder methods for every one of them.

But the one of whom he was most jealous – and for whom he planned the most agonising death – was the one Isadora had met and taken a shine to on their transatlantic voyage.

The bullfighter had his matador's sword with him and he had had a lot of practice in using it. His next encounter with The Honourable Devereux Lyminster would, if El Falleza had anything to do with it, be short and lethal.

So, it was probably just as well that Blotto wasn't staying at the Cactus Flower Hotel. He had been invited to join his sister and enjoy the hospitality of the Guiteras Ranch. Since that involved a great deal of horse-riding and drinking, so far as Blotto was concerned it was all creamy éclair.

Corky Froggett was also happy with his new billet. In the servants' quarters at the back of the General's mansion, he quickly made the acquaintance, to their mutual satis-faction, of a kitchen maid called Carmelita. She was a very organised young lady with a strong taste for men, and also for refried beans, which she cooked at every opportunity. Soon after joining the Guiteras Ranch staff, she had decided she didn't like the stuffy top-floor dormitory where she was meant to sleep with the rest of the maids.

She had therefore explored the estate and found, not far from the house, a small cave. It had been used over the years for waste disposal, but Carmelita used her limited time off work to clear it, hang the walls with curtains and turn the space into a private boudoir. Being underground, the cave was much cooler than the house, and it was there that she entertained a string of lovers, of whom Corky Froggett was the latest (though he didn't know about the others, of course). The space Carmelita had created shared certain qualities with a fairy grotto (not that Corky would have known what a fairy grotto was if it jumped up and bit him on the shin). Though perhaps few fairy grottos smelt as much of refried beans.

It goes without saying that, though the Lagonda had ceded its position as Blotto's primary means of transport to the horses, the chauffeur still defied the Mexican sand and dust with his punctilious cleaning of the car every morning. He did the same with his knee-high black leather boots. Corky Froggett did not let being in a foreign country allow him to drop his standards.

It was on the second day of Blotto's stay at the Guiteras Ranch that Sydney Pollard came to visit. On being told that the young English aristocrat was out riding with his sister, the corned beef magnate asked if he could see the man's chauffeur. Corky Froggett was duly detached from the lubricious arms of Carmelita in her fairy grotto (it was her morning coffee break) and summoned to the stables where the Lagonda was parked. He was, as ever, impervious to foreign heat, dressed in his full uniform, buttoned up to the neck, black leather boots up to his knees, and with his peaked cap firmly in place.

Due to his preoccupation on the transatlantic crossing with the First-Class Dining Room waitress in the linen room, Corky had not seen Sydney Pollard before. He looked at the short, tubby, cigar-smoking figure with some suspicion. The chauffeur was suspicious of anyone who went too close to the precious Lagonda.

'What do you want then?' he asked, without finesse.

'I'm interested in the contents of the Lagonda's secret compartment.'

'The Lagonda doesn't have a secret compartment,' asserted Corky. His understanding of the word 'secret' was that nobody should know about it.

'Oh, I think you'll find it does,' said Sydney Pollard.

The chauffeur, not liking the man's tone, said, 'I've been looking after this car longer than you've been smoking cigars, sonny. And if I say it doesn't have a secret compartment, it doesn't have a secret compartment.'

'There's no point in pretending that—'

'Listen, lard-chops!' There was now no attempt to conceal his aggression. 'I am a highly trained fighting machine and, as such, I was very effective during "the last little dust-up in France". And I have a habit of exercising my homicidal skills against people who disagree with me. Now, suet-slops, are you still telling me there is a secret compartment in this Lagonda?'

Taking the wise decision that discretion was the better part of valour, Sydney Pollard said he would wait until Corky Froggett's young master appeared.

'Begonia's in a bit of a gluepot,' said Twinks.

They had left early from the Guiteras Ranch, aiming to get their ride in before the midday sun reached its full strength. Though, for Blotto, no vista could ever hold a candle to what he saw out of his bedroom window at

Tawcester Towers, he had to admit that the Mexican landscape did boast some splendid sights. The prehistorically craggy mountains, the verdant plains, the dusty scrubland, the giant cacti ... it was all strange ... but wonderful country to ride in. Though the horses provided by the Guiteras Ranch were strong and powerful, Blotto thought wistfully of how Mephistopheles might respond to the conditions.

More urgent, though, was responding to the concern he had heard in his sister's voice. 'Begonia? In a gluepot? What kind of gluepot?'

'The man she's in love with is about to be coffinated by firing squad.'

'Is he, by Denzil? A bit of a candle-snuffer.'

'You can say that with two cherries on.'

'So has the poor pineapple trodden the muddy side of the law?'

'Well, yes, he has, brother of mine. But the law in question is a leadpenny one, forged up specially for the occasion.'

'What, you mean some slugbucket has invented the law simply to coffinate Begonia's slice of redcurrant cheesecake?'

'That's about the right size of pyjamas, Blotters.'

'We must rescue the poor thimble. Quick as a lizard's lick.'

'I agree. Quick as a cheetah on spikes.'

'Quick as two ferrets in a rabbit warren,' Blotto agreed. 'But boddoes who invent leadpenny laws like that deserve to have the full weight of the real laws come crashing down on them. Tarring and feathering's too good for the sponge-worm. So, who's the bucket of bilge-water who's invented this fumacious law?'

'Begonia's father. General Henriquez Guiteras.'

Blotto stopped short. 'Ah. That rather pitches the crud in the crumpet mix, doesn't it?'

'I read your semaphore. The "host" thing?'

'You're bong on the nose there, Twinks me old spat-brush. Doesn't do to go tarring and feathering a boddo when you're enjoying his hospitality.'

'You've potted the black there, Blotters.'

'Broken biscuits!' It was that serious. Scratching his chin in frustration, he went on ruefully, 'Having principles is sometimes a tough rusk to chew, isn't it, Twinks?'

She nodded. Sometimes, being brought up the way they had been did make life very difficult. The slender hope she'd had, that her brother might agree to go against their host's wishes, trickled away. She would have to find some other argument to persuade him.

When they returned to the Guiteras Ranch at the end of their ride, Blotto was immediately confronted by an aggrieved Corky Froggett. 'Milord, there was some toerag came round, suggesting that the Lagonda might have a secret compartment.'

'But, Corkers old man, the old girl does have a secret compartment.'

'You know that, milord. And I know that. But how does the toerag know that?'

This was not a question that Blotto had addressed when it first might have arisen, on his initial encounter with Sydney Pollard. And it was not a question he intended to address now.

'Chubby boddo, was he? Built on the lines of an India rubber ball?'

'That is correct, milord,' said Corky Froggett, his suspicions far from being allayed.

54

'Well, don't don your worry-boots about him. That's Sydney Pollard. He's made of pure brick-mix. Piled up lots of the old jingle-jangle in the corned beef biz and is now up to the wing collar in charity work. The reason he knows about the Lag's secret compartment is because he filled it up with corned beef for the starving children of Mexico. The boddo really is a Grade A foundation stone.'

The Grade A foundation stone in question was found by Blotto in one of the Guiteras Ranch's many terra-cotta courtyards, puffing on another monster cigar and enjoying the General's brandy.

Blotto asked whether he wanted to do the transfer of the goods by the stable where the Lagonda was parked, but Sydney Pollard demurred. 'I do not want it done where anyone might see.'

'Why? Nothing about the Stilton's iffy, is it?'

'Good heavens, no. Whole thing's as straight as a mathematician's ruler. The reason for my secrecy is that I don't do charity work for my own self-glorification. I like to keep quiet about it, so I resist having my name associated with any of my charitable ventures. I prefer for the beneficiaries to glory in the largesse without knowing where it's come from.'

'By Wilberforce, you're really playing the Galahad, Sydney.'

'One does one's best for the less fortunate,' said the modest corned beef magnate.

Blotto drove the open-topped Lagonda, with Sydney Pollard sitting beside him giving directions. Corky

Froggett sat in the back, feeling excluded. He still wasn't convinced about their passenger's credentials as a knight in shining armour. Suspicion came naturally to Corky. On many occasions in his adventures with Blotto and Twinks, it had been justified.

There was not a lot of shelter on the Mexican plains, but Sydney Pollard knew a wooded area, in the shade of which a cart with two mules in harness waited for them. Peons in loose tattered clothes and shabby sombreros lay on the ground around the cart. The air was heavy with the bitter smell of cigarillo smoke.

No one moved until the Lagonda had come to a halt. But when Sydney Pollard got out of the car, it was clear that the group recognised him. A man with long white moustaches rose to his feet in an unhurried manner. But he moved more sharply when Pollard snapped instructions at him in fluent Mexican Spanish. And his dozing minions also woke up at the sound of authority.

Corky Froggett's offers to help move the crates were summarily rejected. Though he spoke none of the local language, he could recognise that the words addressed to him were deeply offensive. He seethed but could do nothing by way of retaliation. He dreamed of having the stenchers in the sights of an Accrington-Murphy machine gun.

The transfer was quickly achieved. The crates of Pollard's Corned Beef were moved from the Lagonda to the back of the mule-cart. Sydney Pollard and the white-moustachioed one sat up at the front, while the peons draped themselves across the crates of donations for the starving children of Mexico.

'Does a boddo good, doesn't it, Corky,' said Blotto, as the Lagonda roared back across the plain, 'to know that he's done a deed on the good side of the egg basket?'

The chauffeur maintained his grumpy silence.

'Right,' said Sydney Pollard, as the driver whipped the recalcitrant mules into action, 'you know where we're going. Don't you . . . Refritos?'

6

Iguana Breeding

A few days passed and very little happened. In the *mañana* culture of Mexico, this was not unusual. Blotto, his brain as ever sublimely unadulterated by thought, enjoyed the horse-riding and the large steaks supplied by the Guiteras Ranch. Twinks was more pensive. She was aware that the *status quo* could not last forever. By declaring the independence of Jalapeno, Colonel Henriquez Guiteras had thrown down a very public gauntlet to the Partido Nacional Revolucionario government. There was no way they could allow him to go unpunished. It was simply a matter of when retribution would follow – and what form that retribution would take.

In the meantime, Twinks fretted about her friend Begonia. Carlos Contreras and his father were, as she had been told, incarcerated in Jalapeno City Jail. She paid a visit there, on the pretence of sight-seeing, and was faced by a building of massive colonial brickwork, guarded by ferocious-looking men in Ruritanian uniforms. Springing anyone from there, though not beyond her capabilities (nothing was beyond Twinks's capabilities), would take a great deal of planning.

But any effort that saved Begonia Guiteras's romantic future would be worthwhile.

So, Twinks, looking convincingly like a tourist (though tourists were a rare sight in Jalapeno), walked casually around the City Jail, committing to memory various dimensions and the location of the building's entrances. Then she sat at a café in the main square, ordered a coffee, and opened the sequined reticule she always carried with her. Taking out a silver-backed notebook and a silver propelling pencil, she committed to paper all the mental notes she had made about the prison.

She also found a helpful source of information in the café's proprietor. Since his business was situated directly opposite the jail, he had had plenty of opportunity to observe the place's daily – and nightly (he stayed open late) – routines. And, like all men, he could not believe the beauty of the exotic creature who had just sat down at one of his tables. He would have told this exquisite angel anything. And he was honoured that she regarded his utterances sufficiently interesting to make notes of them.

The café proprietor, whose name was Diego, was not used to being listened to. His home life was rendered unhappy by a dominant and talkative wife. That was why he kept the café open virtually round the clock. At least, there he had some kind of audience. The fact that it consisted almost exclusively of the local drunks wasn't perfect, but it was better than being at home.

So, to have a listener as beautiful and interested as Twinks fulfilled Diego's wildest fantasies. Whatever he talked about – be it his secret political affiliation to the Partido Nacional Revolucionario or his detailed knowledge of the routines at Jalapeno City Jail (he'd visited many friends incarcerated there during the Mexican civil war) – she seemed to be unfailingly fascinated.

And as he talked, her silver propelling pencil moved faster and faster across the lined pages of her silver-backed notebook.

For the next few days, Twinks was frustrated and bored. Her normal recourse in such a situation was to take on a translation project. To that end, she had brought with her a copy of Cervantes' *Don Quixote* in the original Golden Age Spanish. So far as she could tell, the work had never been translated into Etruscan and, while many people might have been happy to let that state of affairs continue, Twinks wasn't among them. So, she had the relevant dictionaries with her. But, somehow, the enervating atmosphere of Mexico rendered her unwilling to settle down to the task. She required more active activity.

Still, she mustn't forget the main reason why she had travelled so far. She once again contacted Professor Hector Troon-Wheatley.

Willy 'Ruffo' Walberswick was back in the Stygian gloom of the same bar. The armed circle who surrounded El Chipito's table may not have been the same individuals as on the previous encounter, but they appeared to have the same murderous intent. They were in fact the core of the army he had recruited for the Partido Nacional Revolucionario.

Their boss's face formed an evil smile which stretched the pale line of his scar. 'So, Mr Journalist, you are back . . .'

'Yes,' Ruffo confirmed.

'And what do you want from El Chipito this time?'

'The same as I wanted from you last time. Information.'

'Information about what?'

'About when your offensive against General Henriquez Guiteras will start.'

'Persistent little terrier, aren't you?' said the mercenary. 'Well, I'll tell you. My offensive will start when I am ready for it to start.'

'That's not enough,' said Ruffo defiantly. 'You must tell me more!'

The scarred man rose to his feet. 'Are you giving orders,' he asked, 'to El Chipito?'

His encircling desperados also rose to their feet. Ruffo felt rifle barrels pushed from various angles into the middle section of his anatomy.

It was an ugly moment. El Chipito had only to give the signal and Willy Walberswick was a dead man. Ruffo couldn't have been more excited. There was a long silence.

Then the mercenary let out a bark of laughter. 'You are brave, Mr Journalist,' he said. Then, to his gang, 'Come on, let's go and do some target practice!'

Within seconds, the downstairs bar was empty.

Or was it? A figure sidled out of the shadows.

Ruffo turned and saw that it was a woman. Shapely, languorous, with long red hair – a rare sight in Mexico.

'So?' she murmured. 'Who are you?'

'My friends call me "Ruffo".'

'So . . . if I called you "Ruffo", I could be your friend.'

'Sounds a beezer wheeze to me,' he said. 'And what's your name-tag?'

'I am Estrella.'

'Estrella.' Ruffo rolled the word around his tongue. 'Sounds good.'

'You stood up to El Chipito,' the woman said. 'Do you positively like danger?'

'Love it,' said Willy 'Ruffo' Walberswick.

'You sound my kind of man,' the woman purred.

* * *

At the entrance, the two horses were tethered to a metal stake driven into the rocky ground. Being sensible creatures, they had moved out of the sun into the shade at the cave mouth, where they chomped amiably on their nosebags.

Further into the shadow, Twinks was explaining something to Professor Hector Troon-Wheatley. 'There's been some sneaky backdoor-sidling going on here.'

'What do you mean?'

'Look at the floor of the cave, Heckie. Do your peepers pip anything squiffy?'

The Professor had to admit that they didn't.

'It's different from when I last pongled over here.'

'Different? In what way?'

'Set your beadies thataway.' Twinks pointed through the narrow mouth of the cave, down the mountainside to the sandy plain beyond. 'The prevailing wind comes from the east . . .'

'Yes.'

'. . . which means that all the spoffing dust from the plain gets blown in here . . .'

'Yes.'

'. . . but there's less dust today than there was when I last dabbled my dainties in here . . .'

The Professor looked around and nodded slowly. 'You're bong on the nose, Twinks.'

'. . . which would suggest to me that some pee-yous have been in since we were last here.'

'I'm sorry? "Pee-yous"?'

'"Persons Unknown".'

'Ah. On the same page.'

Twinks scrutinised the surface of the cave floor more closely. 'This has been swept with a brush. What does that set blipping in the old braincells?'

Professor Hector Troon-Wheatley looked puzzled. He had an excellent academic brain which could date a shard of pottery to within minutes of its original breakage. But, although archaeology involved a great deal of clue-following, he didn't have the focused mind of a criminal investigator.

Which, of course, Twinks did. 'The reason for sweeping in a cave that is not a spoffing dwelling-place must be to hide traces of sneakery. Some horracious fugworms have been playing the rat's part here.'

The Professor did not respond, aware that he was in the presence of one more knowledgeable than himself.

'If blood had been shed, there'd be traces of it in the sand, so my solutionette would be that something heavy has been dragged across, and the dust-raking was to hide the giveaways. And, Heckie, what do you see on this cave floor that's heavy?'

The Professor looked cautiously around and replied tentatively, 'Nothing.'

'Larksissimo!' crowed Twinks. 'You've winged the partridge with your first shot! Whatever has been dragged across the floor – and the direction of the sweeping shows that the goods have been dragged in rather than dragged out – is no longer perceptible to the peepers. Which means that you're on the right side of right.'

Puzzlement furrowed his noble brow. He still hadn't a clue what she was talking about.

'It means, Heckie, that there definitely is a lower cave structure where the heavy goods have been stored.'

'Oh, jubilation!' cried the archaeologist.

'Your only to-do now is to find the entrance.'

'I've examined every inch of the cave without success,' said the Professor. 'But what you've just said has really lifted my spirits. I'll find that entrance or die in the attempt!'

'Of those two, I think finding the entrance is the option that takes the tiggywinkle,' said Twinks.

'Yes.' Troon-Wheatley looked anxiously towards the daylight. 'I'm worried about being spied on. It is most important – vitally important – that nobody knows what I am doing. What I find at this dig could cement my archaeological reputation internationally. So, no one must find out about it. There are a lot of people who, from a variety of motives, would like to know how to get inside the lower caves.'

'And some boddoes who already do know.'

'Sorry?'

'The dust-sweeping we've just popped our peepers on,' Twinks explained patiently, 'as I've just explained patiently, indicates that someone has gained access to the spoffing lower cave quite recently.'

'Oh yes,' said the Professor. 'On the same page. Anyway, while I search for the hidden entrance, you must keep watch at the cave mouth.'

This was not what Twinks wanted to hear. If there was any adventure going on, she wanted to be part of it. But she curbed her instinctive response of disagreement. The Professor was in charge of the dig; it was his initiative. And her role was just as his helper. So, though it went against her every instinct, whenever he told her to do anything, she must obey.

(Besides, she was also pretty sure, since he'd already tried for a long time to find the entrance without success, it was only a matter of time before he'd have to ask for her help, anyway. And Twinks felt pretty confident she'd find a way of solving the mystery – as she had solved so many other mysteries in the past.)

So, docile, demure and tractable, Twinks went to the cave mouth and sat on the dusty sand beside the horses, with her back against the stone wall. From there, she could not see the recesses of the cave where Troon-Wheatley was conducting his search. Not even a flicker from his electric torch was visible. All was dark.

As Twinks looked out, down the mountainside and over the plain, hearing the chomping in the horses' nosebags and the clink of their harness, she was soon slipping into a drowsy doze.

'I knew I would find you here.' The voice broke into her slumber. 'The woman I am going to marry!'

Though rudely awoken, Twinks instantly had all her wits about her. 'Colonel Pedro Jiminez, you have a brain the size of a rabbit dropping,' she responded coolly. 'Have I not made it clear that I would not marry a blunderhead like you if the alternative was injecting my eyes with sulphuric acid.'

He looked down from the height of his horse. A broad-brimmed leather hat was tipped down over his face and his legs were encased in leather chaps.

'Am I to take that as a "no" then?' he asked.

'You can bet your last plipping poncho it's a "no"!'

'Twinks, I want to take you for a ride,' he said.

'Nobody takes Lady Honoria Lyminster for a ride,' she said glacially.

'I meant merely that you should accompany me on a horse ride. There is something of great interest I wish to show you.'

'I'll bet a guinea to a groat that it's of greater interest to you than it is to me.'

'That remains to be seen.' Suddenly the Colonel became aware of something. 'There are two horses here. Why is that? Is there someone else in the cave, up to no good?'

Twinks thought quickly. Professor Hector Troon-Wheatley had been most insistent about the secrecy of his mission. His international reputation as an archaeologist was at stake.

'Grandissimo, Pedro,' she said. 'I'll come for a horse ride with you. I'm sure it'll be pure creamy éclair.'

Jiminez smiled a confident smile. He knew that, in time, all women succumbed to his abundant charms.

The horse ride took some half-hour. There was little conversation. Colonel Pedro Jiminez made overtures but, having diverted him from muscling in on Troon-Wheatley's dig, Twinks didn't feel any further obligation to be polite to him.

Their destination was visible long before they arrived there. The Colonel led the way in the direction of more mountains and, through the dust, emerged the outline of a long wall. 'This is my property,' he announced proudly. 'The Lazy Iguana Ranch. That is where you will live when you are married to me.'

Twinks hadn't got the energy to argue further. If he was stupid enough to have ignored all her previous put-downs, then he wasn't worth bothering with. And she had achieved her main aim, which was to stop the Colonel from investigating Professor Troon-Wheatley's activities.

The open wooden gates of the Lazy Iguana Ranch were on a substantial scale, too high when closed to be climbed without siege equipment. And the rock-built walls contributed to the sensation that they were entering a fortress. Twinks had had the same thought when she first arrived at the Guiteras Ranch. These properties were run like little fiefdoms and seemed to be prepared for conflict with rival landowners. It made Twinks feel quite nostalgic. That, after all, was how Tawcester Towers had operated during the Middle Ages. And the Lyminsters had long memories for those golden days of the feudal system.

Like General Henriquez Guiteras, Colonel Pedro Jiminez seemed to have a private army. Inside the compound, he was greeted by a scruffy band of cutthroats. He obviously wanted Twinks to be impressed by the respect he was shown, but she refused to oblige. She was determined not to be impressed by anything he offered her.

The Colonel showed her round the house, built in similar style to – but on a smaller scale than – the Guiteras property. Twinks got the feeling that Jiminez had spent his entire life trying – and failing – to match up to his boss. She continued refusing to play his game and offered no commendation for anything he displayed to her at the Lazy Iguana Ranch.

Eventually, he said, 'There is one thing I have not shown you yet – something that I think will impress you . . . terrify you, even.'

'What absolute guff!' she said. 'We Lyminsters don't terrify easily. We came through the Norman Conquest, the Wars of the Roses and the Civil War with our cockades crowing. If you think I'm going to get the chillies from something I see in Mexico, then you're definitely shinny-ing up the wrong drainpipe.'

'We will see,' said Colonel Pedro Jiminez, allowing an evil smile to play around his features. 'Follow me.'

He led her round the back of the house and towards the sheer rockface which functioned as a backdrop to his estate. An area against this wall was cordoned off by a chain-link fence. One side wall of this enclosure was a dilapidated building which appeared to be some kind of lockup. There was a roof of wire netting across the top of the space, to prevent whatever creatures the compound contained from climbing out.

Twinks moved closer to see what it did contain.

'Notice anything unusual about them?' asked Colonel Pedro Jiminez.

'They're big,' said Twinks, a little awestruck in spite of herself. 'By Wilberforce, they're big.'

'Bred to be so,' said the Colonel with undisguised pride. 'You know what they are?'

Of course she did. If he spent more time with her (a possibility which she would do everything in her considerable power to prevent), he would realise that Twinks knew everything.

'They are black iguanas,' she said. 'Also knows as spiny-tailed iguanas or, to use their Latin name, *Ctenosaura similis*. They are the largest species in the genus Ctenosaura. They were first described in 1831 by the British zoologist, John Edward Gray. When hatched from their eggs, the young are green in colour, but they soon turn dark grey or black. Typically, adults grow up to the size of four feet three inches, though the specimens in this compound are considerably larger.'

The Colonel beamed. 'Like I said, skilful breeding.'

'They are enthusiastic climbers,' Twinks went on, 'and are the fastest-moving of all the lizard species. An adult male can reach speeds of more than twenty spoffing miles an hour.'

'Mine can go faster than that. This place may be called the Lazy Iguana Ranch, but my iguanas are far from lazy. I have seen to it that they are specially trained for speed.'

Twinks looked into the compound. There was plenty of evidence for the species' enthusiasm for climbing. Not only were they roaming along the branches of the trees inside their cage, they were also crawling over the wire netting of its walls and roofing. They were, as Jiminez had asserted, extremely large. And, though they were called black, most of their scaly bodies were green, with parallel striations in a darker colour. The spines, which gave them their other name, ran along the ridges of their backs, growing more prominent on their long tails.

'Rum baba that they're green,' said Twinks.

'Something to do with their diet,' said the Colonel mysteriously.

'Well, they're never going to win the rosette in a beauty parade, are they?' Twinks observed. 'They look like monsterbludgeons who'd have your leg off as soon as they'd clapped their peepers on you.'

'Yes, they do,' the Colonel agreed with satisfaction.

'Cheers the soul to know they're herbivorous,' Twinks went on.

'Really?'

'Yes.' She was a little surprised that someone who claimed to breed the species knew so little about them. 'When the infant iguanas are not long out of the shell, they'll eat insects and small animals but, as they mature, they turn strictly veg.'

'Most of them do,' Colonel Pedro Jiminez agreed.

'Sorry, not reading your semaphore?'

'Because the iguanas start their lives as omnivores, it is possible, by limiting their diet to meat, to turn them into lifelong carnivores.'

Twinks was taken aback. 'Well, I'll be kippered like a herring,' she said.

'Watch this!' Jiminez opened a foul-smelling storage box nearby and pulled out the over-ripe carcass of a dog. He opened a feeding hatch in the wire-netting wall and threw the cadaver through.

Instantly, all of the iguanas pounced on their new treat. Those closest bit into the rotting flesh of the dog. Those further away bit into the necks of their speedier colleagues, hoping to get at the prey. Within a minute, nothing remained except a pile of bones.

'See what I mean?' said the Colonel with ill-disguised triumph. 'And, would you believe, there's another tasty morsel they prefer even to a dead dog.'

69

'What is it when it's got its spats on?'

'Some weeks ago,' he began, with an evil smile, 'one of the peons who works on the ranch – the one who looks after and feeds the iguanas – had to go into the compound. He did that regularly, sweeping out the droppings, making it a clean place for the iguanas to live in. But, as he was making his way out with the buckets of droppings, he tripped over his broom and fell.

'Sadly, in falling, he cut his leg. The iguanas responded instantly to the smell of human blood. It enraged them, as it does sharks. Within seconds, they were on to him. The iguanas ate everything – his clothes, his shoes, everything.'

He pointed to the pile of dog bones. 'Like that. Bigger bones, of course, but just like that.'

'Great galumphing goatherds!' said Twinks, impressed.

'And, since that incident,' Jiminez continued slowly, 'the iguanas have changed. They look at us people differently. No longer do they see us just as creatures who bring them food. Now they see us as creatures who could *be* food.'

'You mean . . . ?' said Twinks.

'Yes. I mean that the iguanas have now got a taste for human flesh.'

'Great spangled spiders!' said Twinks.

'Which also means . . . that my iguanas have become a very useful method of persuasion . . . for people who do not do exactly what I want them to do.'

There was no doubt about it. Twinks could recognise a threat when she heard one.

7

The Second Level

There was a clatter of approaching horse hoofs and Twinks looked over towards the main entrance to the Lazy Iguana Ranch. A cloud of dust resolved it into the welcome sight of Blotto riding towards them.

'Hoopee-doopee!' he cried. 'How're your doodles dangling?'

'Larksissimo!' she cried in response. 'I'm in zing-zing condition.'

'I thought you might fancy a stirruping with me across the plippy plains of Mexico.'

'Nothing would fit the pigeonhole better, Blotto me old whalebone corset.' Then, remembering how well brought up she was, 'I don't think you've had the p of meeting Colonel Pedro Jiminez.'

'No, I haven't,' said Blotto, equally well brought up. 'Enormous p to make your a, me old trouser button.'

'*Buenos días*,' said the Colonel, with something less than enthusiasm. Then, unaware of their sibling relationship, he went on, 'You are close to Twinks, yes?'

'"Close"?' echoed Blotto. 'We're as tight as Tam O'Shanter's trews. Few people who've twiddled the marital reef-knot are as close as me and Twinks.'

'Are you married then?' asked Colonel Pedro Jiminez.

'Not yet,' said Twinks with a twinkling laugh. 'And in no hurry to be so. Well, no more fiddling round the fir trees. We must be pongling along.'

And the pair of them galloped off, not knowing that they had left Colonel Pedro Jiminez with the impression that they were engaged to be married. Which only increased the instinctive animus he had felt towards the handsome young Englishman.

Colonel Pedro Jiminez became determined to kill Blotto.

Twinks had been considerably relieved by her brother's arrival. She had no concerns about her ability to escape the clutches of Colonel Pedro Jiminez, but his threat to turn the iguanas on her had put her in something of a flippety-flap. From which it was pure creamy éclair to be extricated. But was Blotto's appearance just coincidence?

It was only when they had ridden out of the Lazy Iguana Ranch that she had a chance to put the question. 'How did you find me, Blotters?' she asked.

'Oh, some boddo back at the Guiteras Ranch said you'd pootled off to see that Loon-Weakly and—'

'Troon-Wheatley.'

'Good ticket. You know who I mean, anyway. They said you were helping him out with his execution and—'

'Excavation.' Twinks was so used to correcting Blotto that such moments hardly interrupted their conversations at all.

'Bong on the nose. So, I pongled off to the cave and saw his horse there, chomping its chow. Couldn't see the archae . . . archae . . . digger boddo. Pongled on to the back of the cave and your Moon-Sweetly came—'

'Troon-Wheatley.'

'Good ticket. Anyway, he came up the stairs.'

'Stairs, Blotto?'

'Yes, stairs from the lower level of the cave.' He had no idea of the importance of what he was saying. 'And I must say, old Spoon-Neatly was—'

'Troon-Wheatley.'

'Good ticket. He looked like the schoolboy who'd been caught by Matron smoking in the San. Face like a rare steak. And he said he'd heard Him 'n' Us talking—'

'Jiminez,' said Twinks patiently.

'Good ticket. And he said Him 'n' Us took you off with him. And your digger boddo seemed keen to get me off the prems, so I pootled over to the Lazy Iguana Ranch where, as you know, I found you.'

'And you were right on the ping with the timing.'

'Sorry, sis. Not on the same page.'

'Let's just say that Colonel Pedro Jiminez was beginning to screw the vice on me.'

'Oh?'

'He's determined I'm going to ding the church bells with him.'

'Don't don your worry-boots about that. Every trousered boddo you meet falls for you like a giraffe on an ice rink. Surely your brainbox has tuned into that by now?'

'Yes, but this particular trousered boddo was cranking up the crisis.'

Blotto was alarmed. 'He didn't hurt you, did he?'

'Not hurt, no. But he did threaten me.'

Blotto pulled hard on the reins and brought his horse to a halt in a clattering of small stones and dust. 'The four-faced filcher!' he cried. 'Fortunately, I've got my cricket bat with me. I'll go back to the Guiteras Ranch quick as a cheetah on spikes to fetch it and then batter the oikish sponge-worm Him 'n' Us from the Oval to Lord's via Edgbaston!'

'No, no, Blotters,' said Twinks. 'Rein in the roans a moment there! There may be a time for battering Colonel Jiminez from the Oval to Lord's via Edgbaston, but it hasn't clocked into the calendar yet. I need more gin-gen about Jalapeno before I can decide who're the Galahads and who're the guthuckets. The politics here are quite complicated.'

'Fair biddles,' said Blotto, losing interest. Her last sentence had contained two words which always made him lose interest, 'politics' and 'complicated'. 'Are you heading back to join Prune-Fleetly?'

'Troon-Wheatley,' said Twinks wearily. 'But I think you've dabbed the digit on the right suggestion. We must pongle back to the Attatotalloss Caves and find out about those stairs you say you saw the Professor coming up.'

'Good ticket,' said Blotto. As was so often the case when his sister made a suggestion, it seemed the only thing to say.

The scene was the same, the subterranean bar. El Chipito was there, surrounded by his army, his sycophantic gang of desperados. The only difference was the person sitting in the chair opposite him. Not Willy 'Ruffo' Walberswick, but Sydney Pollard. The aroma of his cigar was classier than the stench of the hoodlums' cigarillos, but only just.

Oh, and there was one other difference. Draped across El Chipito's knee was the woman called Estrella. Though she was very definitely his, he took as much notice of her as he might of a jacket hung over the back of his chair.

'I will arrange for a map to be sent to you with the precise location,' said Pollard.

'Why not just tell me where the goods are now?' demanded El Chipito.

Without raising his voice, the tubby man repeated, 'I will arrange for a map to be sent to you with the precise location.'

His acolytes tensed at this apparent rudeness, but their boss calmed them with a wave of his hand. Whatever power game was being played out here, it wasn't the predictable one.

'You know,' said El Chipito, 'that hostilities are about to commence?'

'Of course.' Pollard spread his hands wide. 'Why else would I be here?'

'And you know, too, that if you try to double-cross me, you will have signed your own death warrant?'

'I have been issued with death warrants many times.' The chubby shoulders were shrugged. 'And I am still here.'

'Your luck will not last forever, Señor Pollard.'

'It's lasting pretty well so far,' came the serene reply.

On a sudden burst of anger, El Chipito cried, 'Tell me where the goods are hidden!'

'I will arrange for a map to be sent to you with the precise location,' said Pollard evenly.

'We leave! I will not be back here for twenty-four hours!' The mercenary stood up suddenly. Estrella slipped off his lap on to the floor. Without a look at her, he swept out of the bar, his bloodthirsty acolytes in tow.

With a chuckle, and at a more leisurely pace, Sydney Pollard followed them out.

Estrella picked herself up from the floor and dusted herself down.

As she did so, a figure stepped out of the shadows and came towards her. It was Willy 'Ruffo' Walberswick.

Sydney Pollard knew his way around Jalapeno City. He had been there many times and understood its networks, the subtle interweaving of the mildly corrupt with the totally corrupt. So, he had no difficulty in obtaining a horse-drawn carriage and driver to take him out to the Guiteras Ranch. This time, once he had arrived there, he had no interest in Blotto or Corky Froggett. His business was with General Henriquez Guiteras.

He was shown into the presence and accepted the suggested glass of tequila. Then he offered the General exactly the same terms as he'd offered to El Chipito.

In the subterranean bar, Ruffo had ordered a beer for himself. Estrella was on the local, gut-rotting brandy. They looked at each other soupily.

'When you said you liked danger,' she murmured, 'you really meant it, didn't you?'

'Is the King German?' asked Ruffo.

The woman looked puzzled. Possibly, the nationality of the British Royal Family was less of a live issue in Jalapeno City than it was in the Land of the Golden Lions.

'How much do you like danger?' Estrella persisted.

'I like it as much as . . . as much as . . .' He seemed distressingly devoid of similes. 'As much as I like anything,' he concluded feebly, before trying to revive the conversation by asking, 'How much do you like danger?'

'I like it as much . . . as much . . .' Estrella's word-hoard too seemed somewhat depleted. 'As much as . . . well, more than anything else.'

They looked at each with an air of blankness, not to say disappointment. The love of danger which had brought them together required the constant fuel of more danger. When they'd first met, El Chipito might have returned at any moment and found them together. That would have been really dangerous.

But this time he'd announced he wouldn't be back for

twenty-four hours. Thus removing the stimulus of immediate danger.

Willy 'Ruffo' Walberswick and Estrella sipped their drinks and tried not to make eye contact. With no danger on offer, both of them were trying desperately to think of something else they might have in common.

Professor Hector Troon-Wheatley was at the cave mouth, looking anxious. It was clear to him that two dust clouds were approaching and, for him, the fact that there were two signalled potential trouble. It was only when the shapes became recognisable as Twinks and Blotto that he felt reassured.

And then only partially reassured. Twinks was his appointed helper, who had already demonstrated her extensive knowledge of Aztec culture; there was no problem about her presence. But her brother ... ? Troon-Wheatley wasn't aware that Blotto had any particular archaeological academic expertise. (Nor, in fact, was he aware of the generally recognised fact that Blotto had no academic expertise of any kind.) Could Twinks's brother be trusted to maintain the secrecy of what was going on in the Attatotalloss Caves? Particularly as the Professor had seen him come snooping around the area earlier in the day.

But when Troon-Wheatley began to question Blotto's right to be there, his arguments were swept away by the sheer force of Twinks's personality.

'Heckie,' she said, 'we need my bro with us. He's a Grade A foundation stone. And he also has the strength of ten, "because his heart is pure". So, if there's any shifting of gubbins to be done, then Blotto's the man for the mission.'

'Well, there is going to be a bit of heavy lifting ...' the Professor conceded.

'Then – larksissimo! – Blotters fits the pigeonhole!' cried Twinks. And, before Troon-Wheatley could raise any further objections, she went on, 'Anyway, I gather you've found that vital crack in the Golden Egg.'

'I wouldn't go that far,' said the Professor.

'Oh, don't shimmy round the shrubbery,' said Twinks. 'Blotters said he'd seen you coming up some stairs from a lower level.'

Troon-Wheatley had to admit that was true.

'Then how do we crack the code? How do we befuddle the bafflers? How do we solve the Aztec secret?'

'I'll show you, Twinks.'

The Professor, too excited now by the imminent revelation of his discovery to worry about Blotto's presence, led them to the back of the cave.

He focused his electric torch on to an uneven rockface, which looked as if it had been chipped out by manmade tools. 'You talk of an Aztec secret, Twinks,' he said, 'but I'm pretty sure this is the work of a more recent civilisation. The gearing system involved looks to me like the work of a Victorian engineer, rather than anything more ancient. It's a fine bit of work. Hard not to admire it. I really like a good bit of apparatus.'

'So do I,' Blotto enthused. 'Particularly with lots of butter.'

Troon-Wheatley looked on in puzzlement, as Twinks murmured to her brother, '"Apparatus", Blotters. Not "asparagus".'

'Good ticket,' said Blotto.

'Anyway,' said the Professor, 'watch this!'

He grabbed hold of a protruding spur of rock and twisted it a quarter of a turn to the right. There was a sound like the grinding of very large coffee beans and, very slowly, a section of rockface slipped away to reveal an opening the size of a house door. Something glowed softly from inside.

'Where in the name of strawberries does that light come from?' asked Twinks.

'Oh, nothing sinister or magical,' replied the Professor. 'I lit some candles down there. So that I'd have both hands free, without having to hold the torch.'

'Are we going to zapple on down then?'

'Certainly, Twinks. I'll lead the way.'

They could see the steps fairly clearly, but Troon-Wheatley still pointed his torch beam downwards to where Twinks's dainty feet were about to land next. He treated her with an enchanted awe which her brother recognised all too well. Ever since Twinks had emerged from the nursery, Blotto had watched an infinite parade of men falling for her like guardsmen in a heatwave.

As she descended into the lower chamber, Twinks, observant as always to every detail, took in the fact that the staircase was relatively new. Its stone steps did not bear the hollowed-out witness of human tread over many centuries. She would have reckoned the work had been completed within the last fifty years.

The chamber itself, though remarkable for its mere existence, was something of a disappointment. The floor, solid rock dusted with sand, was flat and unrevealing. The walls and ceiling were of stone worn smooth by centuries of time rather than the effects of man-made tools. And, though there were enough prominent rock features to offer the possibility of another secret lever leading to further secrets, basically the space was empty.

Except for one end, where there appeared to have been a rock fall. A cascade of small stones, none much bigger than a man's fist, had sealed off whatever lay beyond. Searching behind the rubble was the obvious next step.

Obvious to Blotto, anyway. With a cry of, 'Hoopee-doopee! No time to fritter! Let's go at this shovel and poker and find out what's under the spoffing dustbin lid!', he hurled himself at the scattered rocks. And started burrowing them out like a dog retrieving a favourite bone.

'Stop! Stop!' cried Professor Hector Troon Wheatley.

Blotto turned back in surprise. 'What's pulled your face down, Heckie?' he asked, automatically using his sister's invented nickname.

'This is a professional excavation site,' said the Professor coldly. 'And it is a site where I am in charge. So, the appropriate protocols must be observed.'

'Tickey-tockey,' said Blotto. 'If I read your semaphore right, you're saying I shouldn't be shifting the gubbins with my hands? I should go up to the next level and get a spoffing pickaxe?'

'No,' said Troon-Wheatley. 'You should desist from doing anything at the moment. You have no academic credentials, do you?'

Blotto admitted he hadn't. He didn't know what an academic credential was.

'At a professional archaeological site,' the Professor went on, 'pieces of stone may not be randomly moved. Each one needs to be documented, numbered, and have its precise location recorded.'

'Oh, come on, Heckie,' said Twinks at her most winsome. (And Twinks's winsomeness had a track record for melting the resolve of the most intransigent officials, heads of state and double-dyed villains.) 'You can see those spoffing stones have been moved within the last few days. They don't need cataloguing.'

'On an excavation site where I am in charge,' said Professor Hector Troon-Wheatley magnificently, '*everything* needs cataloguing.'

Blotto looked at his sister, hoping to read in her expression permission for him to continue dismantling the wall of stone.

But he was out of luck. Meekly, Twinks said, 'You're on the right side of right, Heckie. So, what's next on the to-do?'

'We close up this lower level of the caves again. We return to where we are staying. I will gather together the necessary equipment for cataloguing the stones. And we will return at eight a.m. tomorrow morning to excavate the site in the appropriate manner.'

'Fair biddles,' said Twinks, still meek. 'Then that's what we'll do.'

As they left the cave complex, Blotto looked at his sister in bewilderment. Meek was not a mood in which he had often seen her before.

But he reassured himself that Twinks was planning something. Knowing her from birth had made Blotto realise that Twinks was always planning something.

8

Corned Beef?

In a run-down shed not far from the Guiteras Ranch, the gangmaster Refritos stroked his white moustaches before settling down to work. Though perhaps it wasn't work, more of a hobby. Certainly, something he enjoyed doing. Something he would have done even if he didn't make money from it.

So, whenever he didn't need to be out organising a labour force, he worked away contentedly in his shed.

He had designed the components himself and made them at his own forge, the other side of the dusty space from the rustic bench at which he was now working. Each half of the structure was shaped like a full-bodied funnel, its top part rounded in outline rather than triangular. When welded together, the two parts made a round ball with tubes sticking out either end. The surfaces of the metal were crisscrossed with furrows to aid fragmentation.

Refritos had been through the construction process so often that he didn't have to think about it. His hands moved automatically. He fixed a percussion cap to seal the end of one tube. Then, using a narrow tin funnel, he poured in the gunpowder until it filled the space inside, right up to the top of the open tube. The open end was then sealed with a second percussion cap and another Refritos Grenade was completed.

He put it into the wooden frame in the crate specially designed to hold ten of the weapons and moved on to make the next one.

Refritos found the work satisfying. He felt good about the contribution he was making to the business of warfare.

And, in deciding which side he should sell the grenades to, he followed the practice of his mentor, Sydney Pollard. He would sell them to both.

When they returned to the Guiteras Ranch that evening, Twinks was distressed to find Begonia in tears. Not seeing her in any of the public courtyards, she had gone upstairs and tapped on the door of her friend's bedroom.

Initially, there was no response. It was only after Twinks had identified herself that she was admitted. On greeting her, Begonia wailed, 'It is terrible! My father has moved the whole schedule forward!'

'Sorry, not reading your semaphore. What schedule?'

'The execution of Carlos and his father. They are to face the firing squad tomorrow morning at dawn!'

Twinks had invited Blotto along to the confab on her balcony. Though actual planning did not feature among his life skills, he was very good at carrying out plans devised by someone else (particularly by his sister). He moved a couple of cats off a chair and joined the two girls.

Begonia was explaining the reasons for her father's change of schedule. 'He knows that the forces of the Partido Nacional Revolucionario are massing and will soon go on the attack. He thinks the death of their representative, General Ignacio Contreras, will affect their morale. Loyalties in this country are extremely volatile. Soldiers on either side in any conflict will readily defect if they think their opponents are gaining the upper hand.'

'Just rein in the roans there for a moment,' said Blotto. 'There are two boddoes in the Jalapeno clinkbox, are there?'

'Yes. General Ignacio Contreras and his son Carlos.'

'But there's only one of them you want to twiddle up the reef-knot with – am I right?'

'Yes.'

'And which one would that be?'

'Carlos,' Begonia replied in bewilderment. 'The General is the same age as my father.'

'Ah. On the same page,' said Blotto. 'Usually a fruitier crumb to share an umbrella with someone round your own vintage.'

'Yes,' agreed Begonia, still confused. She hadn't spent long enough in Blotto's company to get used to his little mannerisms.

'Anyway,' said Twinks, in a voice of hearty reassurance, 'don't don your worry-boots, Beggers. Your Aged P is not the only one who can move his schedule up.'

'Sorry? What do you mean?'

'Since I've been here, I've been knitting in my noddle a way of springing the two Contrerases out of Jalapeno City Jail.'

'Oh, Twinks . . .' Begonia brought her hands to her face in relief.

'I'd clocked it into the calendar for a week or so hence, but the plan's all in zing-zing condition, so it's just a matter of squeezing the trigger a tidge earlier.'

'Just a momentette . . .' said Blotto.

'What, Blotters me old elastic-sided boot?'

'We chewed the breeze about this some days ago. Talked about springing these poor thimbles from the clinkbox. And then it blipped the braincells that we couldn't do it while we were enjoying the hosp of the boddo who put them there.'

'Ah, yes.'

'Sorry, Twinks. Bit of a candle-snuffer, I agree.'

'Well, it would be,' she agreed. 'But we're not back in the Land of Golden Lions now. We're in Mexico. And . . .' The azure eyes sought out Begonia's brown ones '. . . I believe society protocol in Mexico about the correct way of behaving towards one's host is a completely different hand of bananas.'

Her friend caught on at once to what she was being asked for. 'Oh yes,' she said. 'Here in Mexico, we follow the "Camarones a la Diabla" protocol.'

'And what's that when it's got its spats on?' asked Blotto.

'It is a time-honoured tradition in our country,' Begonia improvised wildly, 'which insists that yes, you must not go against the wishes of the person whose hospitality you are enjoying . . .' She racked her brain for inspiration. 'Unless . . . Unless . . . your host's first name is Henriquez.'

Begonia looked at Twinks apologetically. She knew it was a feeble conclusion which nobody with half a brain would believe.

But she had underestimated – or perhaps overestimated – Blotto's intellectual prowess. 'Tickey-tockey,' he said, instantly satisfied. 'So, as long as we're on your Pater's prems, we can do what we spoffing well like.'

'You've potted the black there, Blotters,' said Twinks. 'So, now we can zap on with the Jalapeno City Jail rescue plan.'

'Are you planning to break into the prison yourself?' asked Begonia breathlessly.

'Not in a month of Wednesdays,' said Twinks. 'But cometh the hour, cometh the man.'

She looked at her brother. Blotto turned round and squinted through into the darkened bedroom behind him. 'Sorry, sis? Who's coming? Who is this man?'

'You are, Blotters.'

'Me coming?' he said, his fine brow knotted. 'But I'm already here.'

It wasn't a job for horse-riding. They would need the Lagonda. And they'd need Corky Froggett too.

A messenger was sent to the servants' quarters and the chauffeur was extracted from the embrace of the kitchen maid called Carmelita. If he was disappointed at the interruption, he was far too well-trained to show it. The abiding principle of Corky Froggett's life was: when the young master calls, the summons must be answered instantly.

Twinks was confident that the late-night carousing at the Guiteras Ranch would be noisy enough for no one to hear the Lagonda driving away from the stable block. And so it proved. But they took the extra precaution of not putting on the headlights. The moon was generous enough for the car to get well away from the Guiteras estate before they needed to switch them on.

Blotto, who was driving, made to turn on to the road to Jalapeno City, but his sister stopped him. 'No, Blotto me old soap dish, we have another to-do before the prison-springing.'

'Toad-in-the-hole!' he said. 'And what is that when it's got its spats on, Twinks me old sock-darning mushroom?'

'We're going to do a little undocumented excavation.'

'Hoopee-doopee!' said Blotto.

* * *

Needless to say, Twinks had three electric torches in her sequined reticule. And she'd seen to it that the requisite shovel and pickaxes were stored in the Lagonda's boot before they left the Guiteras Ranch. Just in case the ones abandoned at the Attatotalloss Caves had somehow been moved.

The journey there was uneventful. Blotto knew the way by now, the winding climb up the mountain towards the entrance. And Corky Froggett was far too professionally buttoned-up to ask any question about their destination. If the young master and the young mistress wanted something to happen, it was his duty to see that it happened. His but to do or die (preferably the latter – though, disappointingly, that ambition had yet to be realised).

On arrival, Twinks knew exactly what was required. Entering the ground-level cave, she walked straight towards the hidden lever on the wall and turned it. The secret opening opened. If Corky Froggett was impressed or surprised by the machinery, he was too restrained to show it. His chauffeurly face remained as impassive as ever.

The candles on the lower level had been extinguished by Professor Hector Troon-Wheatley before he left the site but, extracting a box of safety matches from her sequined reticule, Twinks reignited them. Blotto and Corky Froggett, armed with pickaxes and shovels, moved towards the wall of rubble.

'Erm, Twinks me old carpet-beater . . .' said Blotto, 'do we have to get the gubbins back exactly as it was?'

'Sorry, not on the same page, Blotto me old horseshoe-hurler.'

'Well, if your boddo Croon-Sweetly—'

'Troon-Wheatley.'

'Good ticket. Well, if he's going to initial every pebble, surely he'll want them put back in the same order as—?'

'Don't don your worry-boots about that, Blotters. Just dig away!'

Her brother needed no second invitation. Nor did Corky Froggett. With pickaxes and shovels, they made short work of clearing the rubble. And very quickly revealed that, as Twinks had suspected, the blocking of the cave had been organised very recently.

Because what the cleared stones revealed was a pile of wooden crates, on whose sides were stencilled the words: 'Pollard's Corned Beef – That's the Stuff to Give the Troops!'

Blotto, who'd never subscribed to the popular prejudice against stating the obvious, stated, 'Corned beef!'

'Do you really think so, Blotters?'

'Of course I do, O sister mine. I only transported this load of gubbins from New York to Mexico in the Lag. You know, in the secret compartment.'

'Did you? Why?'

'Because, sis, Sydney Pollard asked me to. And I've always been a bit of a limp-rag when people ask me to do to-dos for charity.'

'And what charity is this lot for?' demanded Twinks.

'It's to bring corned beef to the starving children of Mexico,' Blotto recited devoutly.

'Is it? Forty thou to a fishbone I know what's in these crates. And I don't think it's got much to do with beef, corned or otherwise.'

Twinks reached into her sequined reticule and produced a crowbar. She hooked it under the lid of the nearest crate and applied pressure. With the sound of reluctant splintering, the lid flew off and landed in a clattering of stones.

'So, Blotters . . .' Twinks pointed into the crate. 'Take a look at what the starving children of Mexico are going to get!'

88

Inside the crate, packed neatly in rows, were a large number of rifles and a couple of machine guns. All manufactured by the premier English firearms company, Accrington-Murphy.

9

Sprung!

Blotto's temper was taunted by the discovery. The fact that he had been so shamelessly duped by Sydney Pollard, the fact that he had been made an unwitting accomplice in the crime of gun-running, really rankled with him. His first instinct was, regardless of the time, to go and wake up the oikish sponge-worm in the Cactus Flower Hotel and have it out with him. And to think that Pollard was English! That only made the situation worse.

But Twinks reminded her brother that there was a more pressing task on that night's agenda. If General Ignacio Contreras and his son Carlos were still in Jalapeno City Jail at dawn the following morning, they would be facing a firing squad.

Diego the café proprietor had been well briefed by the vision of extraterrestrial loveliness who had paid his humble establishment a second visit earlier in the day. The contrast between the Englishwoman and his wife back home had become positively painful.

When they arrived that night, Twinks directed Blotto to the yard behind the café, where Diego had assured her they would be unobserved. By arrangement, the café proprietor joined them in the Lagonda for her final briefing.

Needless to say, he did not speak or understand English, but Twinks, whose Mexican Spanish was as good as the other hundred-odd languages she was fluent in, translated smoothly for him.

Issuing the instructions so near the event was a deliberate tactic on her part. Much as she adored her brother, Twinks had no illusions about his skills when it came to the grasp of detail. Unless the subject was one dear to him – in other words, cricket or hunting – his brain had the retentive capacity of a colander. But he could immediately activate any directive the moment it was delivered. And, in case Blotto did get muddled, Corky Froggett was present as a back-up. His ability to commit detailed orders to memory had been finely honed during 'the last little dust-up in France'.

First, Twinks extracted some useful objects from her sequined reticule and gave them to Blotto and Corky. 'And there's one Spanish word you must remember, Blotto. In case the prisoners think you're going to coffinate them. Just say, "Salvador". It means "rescuer". Then they'll know you're on the good side of the egg basket.'

'Hoopee-doopee!' said Blotto. '"Salvador".'

'Bong on the nose, bro!'

'Good ticket.'

Then Twinks said, in a voice that brooked no argument, 'Right, time to put a jumping cracker under it! If you do exactly what I tell you to do, it will all be creamy éclair.'

The moonlight bathed everything in pale magic. Blotto and Corky Froggett waited in the shadowed entrance of

Diego's café. They watched as the two Ruritanian-uniformed guards, rifles on their shoulders, crossed in front of the prison gates and exchanged a ribald greeting in Spanish without breaking stride, each going the opposite way around the building. As Diego had observed many times and Twinks had checked earlier in the day, it took them fourteen-point-seven seconds till they reached their respective corners. Then there was a forty-eight-point-three-second window while both guards were out of sight of the gates.

As the two guards turned on their way to the back of the building, Twinks hissed, 'Skiddle!'

Young master and devoted chauffeur, as instructed, skiddled across the road between the café and the prison. Outside the main gates, Blotto, his sister's instructions freshly planted in his mind, shoved his elbow into the topmost panel of the right-hand door, just as Diego had observed the guards doing on a daily basis. Predictably enough, as they had for the guards, the doors opened.

Inside the prison, there was no sound except for heavy snoring from the ground-floor guardroom where, again as Diego had foretold, the resident staff were all out for the count. The empty wine bottles on the table bore witness to what had speeded them towards slumber (though the drugs which had hastened that process could, of course, not be seen). Hanging on a row of hooks just inside the door was the anticipated ring of cell-door keys and a smaller ring of others. Blotto removed them with great caution, ensuring that there was no clinking of metal.

The two Englishmen climbed softly up the stairs, turning right on the first landing and counting their way along the cell doors. Through the small barred opening in each one came the grunting and grumbling of its sleeping occupant. From the cell at the end came the sounds of two male voices whispering frantically in Spanish. But then the prospect of facing a firing squad within hours would make most people whisper frantically in any language.

It was fortunate that the door keys were numbered. As Blotto turned the relevant one in the lock, the voices ceased. And as the door opened inward, the two Contrerases were revealed. They stood proudly, side by side, defying whatever fate had in store for them. The expressions on their faces, the grizzled one of the General and the smooth one of his son, looked heroic and combative, ready to fight the invaders. But the shackles on their wrists and ankles, chained to rings on the stone floor, rendered any kind of aggressive movement impossible.

'Don't don your worry-boots,' Blotto whispered. Then, triumphantly, 'Stevedore!'

'Salvador, milord,' Corky Froggett murmured.

'Good ticket.'

Whether it was the spoken word that did it, or the fact that Blotto proceeded to unlock their chains with keys from the smaller ring, the two Contrerases were instantly ready to cooperate. The four moved silently back downstairs.

The snoring from the guardroom continued evenly, while they waited by the front gates for the next ribald exchange between the outside custodians. The escape group rounded the fourteen-point-seven seconds up to sixteen, before opening the door and skiddling across to the café. Long before their forty-eight-point-three-second window had closed, the escapees were in Diego's back yard and the two Contrerases were being stowed in the secret compartment of the Lagonda.

'Where do we zapple off to now, O sister of mine?' asked Blotto, once he was installed in the driver's seat. 'Where are we going to shuffle away the suspects?' Twinks had very wisely not overloaded his brain capacity with information about what would happen after the springing from prison had been achieved.

'We drive back to the Guiteras Ranch, O brother of mine.'

'But isn't that rather prodding a red-hot poker into the hornets' nest?' asked Blotto. 'Making it easy for the Contrerases to be jammed in the jug again?'

'No, in the name of snitchrags, Blotters. If the Lag is back at the ranch by three in the morning, General Henriquez Guiteras's blunderthugs will just think we've been lighting up the fireworks of fun somewhere. If it's not back by the morning, they'll get a whiff that the Stilton's iffy.'

'Toad-in-the-hole!' said Blotto admiringly. 'You do think of everything, Twinks me old rust remover.'

It was nearly three by the time the Lagonda nosed its way back to the space behind the Guiteras Ranch stables. The sounds of revelry from the main house had not abated and this time the car's headlights were proudly blazing. They positively wanted their return to be observed. The automatic assumption would be that they had been carousing elsewhere.

There was a moment of alarm when, as the Lagonda came to a halt, a figure detached itself from the shadows of the stables and came towards them. But the panic was short-lived when the moonlight revealed Begonia.

'I am sorry,' she whispered, 'but I must see Carlos.'

'Don't don your worry-boots about him,' said Twinks. 'Your slice of redcurrant cheesecake is in zing-zing condition.'

'But I must *see* him,' Begonia pleaded.

Blotto demurred. 'Having got the poor greengages here, we don't want to risk anyone else clapping their peepers on them.'

'Blotto,' said his sister imperiously, 'hold back the hounds a moment. Do you not care a tuppenny farthing for the feelings of a woman in love?'

'Well, erm . . .' was all he could come up with by way of response.

'Have you never seen a woman in love, Blotters?'

'I'm not sure that I have,' he replied cautiously.

(Of course, he had seen women in love many times. Most fell in love just at the sight of him. But having been brought up in the way he had, and having been to the public school he had, as has been established, the idea that he might be attractive to the opposite sex had never occurred to him.)

'What does a woman in love do?' he went on. 'Just moon and mawk?'

Not for the first time, ignoring his question, Twinks took over. 'Corky,' she demanded, 'open the secret compartment!' The chauffeur did as requested. 'Begonia, get in the car.'

The scene was a touching one. The removal of the secret compartment's covering revealed the Contrerases, father and son, lying side by side, like effigies on a tomb. Their initial alarm at being seen vanished as the son saw who was looking down at him.

'Begonia,' he murmured, with all the love that a young man in his twenties can muster.

'Carlos,' she breathed back at him, with her equivalent store of love. Then, remembering her manners, she added, 'Good evening, General Contreras.'

'*Buenas noches*,' said the father.

Both Contrerases now moved, attempting to emerge from their sanctuary.

'I'd keep your tall poppies below the parapet,' Blotto advised. 'Don't want to be peepered by any of the Guiteras blunderthugs.'

Father and son lay back down, as instructed.

Then Carlos asked, in perfect English, 'Begonia, will you marry me?'

'Of course,' she replied. 'Of course I will marry you, Carlos.'

In spite of their unusual relative postures, the young couple, their faces silvered by moonlight, managed to effect a kiss.

Twinks thought, as romantic moments went, that was the panda's panties.

Blotto thought it was a bit treacly for his taste.

And, if Corky Froggett thought anything, he certainly didn't show it.

How thoughtful for that specific audience, Twinks also thought, for them to have conducted the proposal in English.

10

Blotto Takes Action

Twinks had given her brother firm instructions as to what he should do in the morning. The next stage of her plan was straightforward. But then she slightly niggled him by adding, 'And don't do anything else, Blotters.'

'What do you mean – "else"? What "else" did you think I was going to do – blow up the Jalapeno City Jail?'

'I wouldn't put it past you, brother of mine.'

'Well, I'll have you know, sister of mine,' he said with wounded dignity, 'that, as a boddo, I'm entirely grown-up and have a very efficient noddle screwed into my neck-socket. I'm quite capable of making my own decisions.'

Past history had showed this to be demonstrably untrue, but Twinks didn't think it was the moment to take issue with him. 'Just, please, don't put a fox in the fairy-ring, Blotters,' she said.

Colonel Pedro Jiminez was not a man to take a slight lightly, and he very definitely felt he had been slighted the previous day. Twinks had not treated him with the respect and awe he thought he deserved, but that was a minor irritation. She was just a woman and he knew it was simply a matter of time before any woman would bend to his iron will.

Her brother's slighting of him, however, was a different matter. Though Twinks could readily have explained them to him, Blotto had no familiarity with the Spanish concepts of *machismo* and *caballerosidad*. So, he didn't realise the extent to which his behaviour towards Jiminez had offended the other's masculine pride.

And he certainly wasn't aware how closely the Colonel followed his movements the following morning. Or how assiduously – though at a discreet distance – the Colonel's red Hispano-Suiza followed the Lagonda into Jalapeno City.

Blotto had never heard the expression 'counter-intuitive' and, if he had, he wouldn't have understood it. But there didn't seem a great deal of logic to the instructions Twinks had given him. General Ignacio Contreras and Carlos Contreras had, after all, been sprung from Jalapeno City Jail and secreted in the Lagonda round the back of Diego's café. If there was any investigation into their abduction by the henchmen of General Henriquez Guiteras, surely it would be centred initially on the area near the prison. In other words, close to Diego's café, particularly since the General's spies probably knew of the owner's dubious loyalties.

And yet Blotto's sister had told him to drive the Lagonda back to exactly the place where the two escapees had been loaded into its secret compartment the night before.

Still, long experience of Twinks's stratagems had taught Blotto the wisdom of going along with them. Rarely had doing so left him holding the wrong end of the sink plunger.

Following her instructions, therefore, in the sheltered

area behind Diego's café, he once again brought the Lagonda to a halt. He had travelled without Corky Froggett; from the perspective of any outside observers, he was alone in the great car.

Clearly also well briefed by Twinks, Diego appeared at the moment of the Lagonda's arrival. He helped the two stowaways out from the secret compartment and led them, along with Blotto, through a small door in a shabby wall whose paint no longer qualified as whitewash.

The door opened on to a dimly lit passage which soon became a steep staircase, leading down into a dimly lit bar. Willy 'Ruffo' Walberswick would have recognised the venue for his meetings with El Chipito, but of course Blotto had never been there before. Nor had he had the p of making the a of El Chipito.

That deficiency was quickly remedied. Diego made the introductions, after El Chipito had clasped the two Contreras, father and son, to his bosom with a Latin enthusiasm which seemed excessive to Blotto. English boddoes – particularly if they had been to public school – didn't do much in the way of clasping each other ... or hugging or any of that rombooley. Ignacio and Carlos Contreras were then passed around the assembled armed desperados for further clasping.

El Chipito looked at the Englishman with suspicion. Blotto looked at the Mexican's facial scar with great interest. The only one he'd seen like it transversed the face of one of his old muffin-toasters from Eton, a poor thimble by the name of Snuffy ffortescue (with one voiced and one silent 'f'). The occasion of his disfigurement had been on the cricket pitch, at the Eton and Harrow match, where a particularly vicious bouncer from Squiggy Ollerenshaw (Harrow) had smashed the stumps with such force that a flying shard of wood had sliced down Snuffy's face with the neatness of a waiter at Rules filleting a Dover sole.

Blotto's keenness to ask El Chipito whether he had also gained his scar in a cricketing accident was interrupted by the mercenary asking him, 'You come from the Guiteras Ranch. Whose side are you on?'

There was only one possible answer for a boddo who had been through the English public school system. 'I am on the side of truth and justice,' Blotto replied.

'Huh,' El Chipito sneered. 'Truth and justice don't have much place in the realities of warfare.'

'Well, those are the spoffing values for which the Lyminster family have always borne the banner. You have only to cast your peepers over our record in the Norman Conquest, the Wars of the Roses, the Civil War and—'

It was fortunate that Blotto was interrupted at this point. Whatever slops he might have been fed in the nursery about the family history, the Lyminsters' record in any of the conflicts he mentioned would not have stood up to scrutiny. Like most English aristocrats, Blotto's dynasty had only ever entered wars from motives of personal profit.

The words of El Chipito which cut him off were: 'But why are you, an Englishman, here in Jalapeno?'

'I pongled over here with one of me old muffin-toasters from Eton. Greengage called Ruffo Walberswick.'

The mercenary nodded. 'I know this man. He is a journalist. Are you also a journalist?'

'Great Wilberforce, no! One of the beaks at Eton said my written English would disgrace a bubba in nursery-naps.'

'So, I ask again, why are you here in Jalapeno?'

'Came to be reunited with Twinks.'

El Chipito's bisected brow furrowed. '"Twinks"? What is a "Twink"?'

'Young boddo of the feminine persuasion. Currently hitching her horses at the Guiteras Ranch.'

'Ah. And you love this "young boddo"?'

'Do the French like cheese?' asked Blotto. 'Always loved her like a pike loves troutlings.'

Not having had the precise nature of Blotto's relationship to Twinks explained, El Chipito automatically assumed that the woman the young Englishman insisted he loved was Begonia Guiteras. The woman the mercenary leader had marked as his own (to join Estrella in his private harem).

El Chipito became determined to kill Blotto.

His blissfully unaware quarry emerged from the subterranean bar, blinking at the ferocious sunlight. He got into the Lagonda and drove it round to park directly in front of the Cactus Flower Hotel.

Blotto knew that, by not going straight back to the Guiteras Ranch, he was disobeying his sister's specific instructions. She had forbidden him, after handing over the Contreras father and son to El Chipito from 'doing anything else'. And 'anything else' was exactly what he was about to do.

Blotto's belief in 'truth and justice' had been severely challenged by the activities of Sydney Pollard. Having met the boddo in all good faith in the First-Class Lounge of their transatlantic liner, Blotto had been totally convinced by the tubby man's story about bringing much-needed corned beef to the starving children of Mexico. To say yes to the suggestion of ferrying those charitable donations in the secret compartment of the Lagonda had been instinctive. But the subsequent discovery that he had been an unwitting accomplice in the business of gun-running had caused him considerable anguish.

If there was any downside to Blotto's generally sunny disposition, it was that his first assumption about people was that they shared his own unshakable belief in truth and justice. Until proved wrong, he was even prepared to extend that assumption to foreigners. As a result, his life featured a sequence of disappointments.

He wasn't worried about the legal ramifications of his Lagonda being used for the purpose of smuggling armaments. From the Norman Conquest onwards, the Lyminster family had been of the view that laws were invented to be observed by other, lesser people. But the fact that Sydney Pollard, an Englishman, could prove to have been so duplicitous caused Blotto almost physical pain. He felt he needed to confront the four-faced filcher and give Pollard a piece of his mind (never, in Blotto's case, an over-generous gift).

An air of lethargy hung around the reception area of the Cactus Flower Hotel. No staff were visible. A quick look in the bar and dining room showed no sign of occupation in either. Reasoning, with rare acuity, that in a two-storey building the bedrooms must be upstairs, Blotto bounded up to the first-floor landing. There were six doors, two for rooms facing the front, four for those facing the back. Sydney Pollard must be in one of them.

He chose one in the front of the building. Knocking and opening the door at the same time, Blotto entered.

And found himself facing the back view of a woman undressed to the waist.

'Good morning, Blotto. How extremely pleasant to see you,' murmured Isadora del Plato.

Colonel Pedro Jiminez had parked up his Hispano-Suiza within view of the back entrance to Diego's café. He knew the Lagonda had to come out that way and idled away the waiting time smoking cigarillos.

When Blotto, blithely unsuspicious of surveillance, drove the great car out, Jiminez eased the Hispano-Suiza into motion to follow him and parked within sight of the Cactus Flower Hotel.

Then he lit another cigarillo. Having become determined to kill the young Englishman, it was now simply a matter of when.

Isadora del Plato had pulled a black lace shawl around her upper body before she turned to face Blotto. Its flimsy texture would not have hidden much from a prurient eye. But neither of Blotto's eyes was even vaguely prurient. Being in the presence of a semi-naked woman was simply embarrassing, not the sort of gluepot that any Old Etonian boddo would wish to find himself in. During their ensuing conversation, he made a very deep study of his well-polished brogues.

'So, Blotto,' Isadora susurrated, 'you have come to give me the dirt, yes?'

'Sorry, Izzy? Not on the same page,' he mumbled.

'I asked you, when we were crossing the Atlantic, if you would keep an eye on what goes on at the Guiteras Ranch. Which I assume is what you have been doing. I also assume you have now finally returned to report to me.'

'Ah. Well. Erm. Good ticket,' he responded.

'You see, Blotto, I deal in information. That is my skill. I gather information from many sources, and I sell to whoever requires it. I am a particularly useful person to know at the time of an "international incident". I know everything that is going on with both sides here in Jalapeno. I know everything about Jalapeno. I know when the war will start and I have a pretty good idea of who is going to win.'

'And you say you sell this information, like a butcher sells chitterlings?'

'Yes, Blotto.' Isadora del Plato smiled at him archly. 'But to certain, favourite, people, I *give* information. I would give information to you, Blotto. Any time. You have only to ask.'

'That's very British of you,' he said. 'Though, of course, the way this particular pint of milk spills, you're not British. Perhaps I should have said, "That's very Spanish of you."'

Further discussion of this ticklish point of etiquette was interrupted by Isadora del Plato's toucan flying in through the window. It perched on the arm of her chair. Deftly, she removed the metal cylinder from its leg and extracted the contents. Another sheet of thin paper with spidery writing, which she read with satisfaction.

'Good,' she announced. 'Both sides have got their armaments in place.'

Blotto wasn't sure what the correct response to this was, so he hazarded a 'Hoopee-doopee!'

Clearly, it hadn't been the wrong thing to say, because the flamenco dancer turned to him and asked, 'So, tell me, Blotto. Now that General Henriquez Guiteras has sourced his weapons, when is he planning to start his offensive against the forces of the Partido Nacional Revolucionario?'

'I haven't a mouse-squeak of an idea,' said Blotto. 'But do you know who the slugbucket is who has been supplying those weapons?'

'Yes, of course,' Isadora replied casually. 'Sydney Pollard.'

'But the lump of toadspawn assured me the crates were full of corned beef,' Blotto protested. 'Whereas in fact they were loaded to the gunwales with Accrington-Murphy's finest.'

Isadora del Plato shook her magnificent mane of black hair. 'I have no idea what you are talking about.'

'Sydney Pollard has a fumacious plan to sell General Guiteras down the river for a handful of winkle shells. The bucket of bilge-water's acting way beyond the barbed wire. Do you know – he's also offering to sell slug-shifters to the government forces!'

'So?' Isadora del Plato, unsurprised, shrugged her magnificent shoulders. 'This is the way of war. Everything has a price.'

'Well, I don't!' said Blotto, also magnificent in his way.

'No?' Suddenly, Isadora del Plato stood up. She moved in front of Blotto, so close that only the flimsy covering of black lace separated her naked flesh from the tweed of his manly chest. 'So . . .' she breathed intimately, 'if I were to offer you all the libido I possess, might I perhaps have found your price, Blotto?'

'I don't think that would actually ping the partridge, Izzy.'

'Why ever not?'

'Well, not to shimmy round the shrubbery, I don't think the libido is legal tender in Mexico.'

'Ooooh . . .'

'It certainly isn't back in England,' said Blotto.

Through the open door on the upper floor of the Cactus Flower Hotel, from the bed on which he lay in truculent mood, the lovesick bullfighter saw Isadora's visitor leave her room. The sight, rather appropriately, was like a red rag to a bull.

El Falleza became even more determined to kill Blotto.

His potential quarry was not aware of the bullfighter's scrutiny. Because, emerging on to the landing, Blotto had seen Sydney Pollard going down the staircase in search of breakfast. Since confronting the gun-runner was the main purpose of his visit to the Cactus Flower Hotel, he swiftly followed.

Sydney Pollard had just taken a seat in the dining room when his nemesis caught up with him

'Now listen, you wretcher!' Blotto began, in righteous fury. 'You're a sneaky backdoor-sidler! And you've been playing a diddler's hand!'

This tirade had little effect on the tubby man, who lit another casual cigar and said to the approaching lethargic waitress, 'Coffee, eggs and beans!' Then, turning to his attacker, 'You want coffee, eggs and beans, Blotto?'

Good manners were too ingrained to prevent the reply being, 'Oh, that's spoffing generous of you. Thanks, Syd.'

'Make that twice,' said Pollard to the waitress. 'And make sure the beans are only fried once!'

'Now what's this about?' asked Sydney Pollard, as wise and conciliatory as a schoolteacher breaking up a play-ground scuffle.

'It's about your being a four-faced filcher,' replied Blotto apologetically, having lost some of his initial impetus.

'Ah. And in what way might I be described as that?'

'In the way any lump of toadspawn could be, if the slugbucket used the cover of charity for the horracious crime of gun-running!'

'And what kind of apology for a human being would do that?' asked Sydney Pollard, all innocence.

'You have done that!'

'I don't think so.'

'Yes, you spoffing well have! You persuaded me, on our transatlantic voyage, to hide your fumacious crates in my Lag, pretending they contained corned beef. Why, in the name of ginger, did you do that?'

'Because I thought,' Pollard replied, reasonably enough,

'if I said the crates contained guns, you wouldn't have taken them.'

'You're coffinating right I wouldn't have taken them!'

'Incidentally,' asked the tubby man, 'how did you find out the crates contained guns?'

'We looked at them in the spoffing caves.'

'Right,' said Pollard thoughtfully. 'And you think I had the guns brought over to sell them to the warring factions in the forthcoming Jalapeno War?'

'What else is there for a boddo to think?'

'In fact,' came the slow reply, 'I brought those guns over to help the starving children of Mexico.'

'Oh, you're jiggling my kneecap. Do you take me for a total voidbrain?'

The answer was of course 'Yes', but Sydney Pollard was shrewd enough to say 'No'.

He went on, 'You're right, Blotto. Those armaments – those fine Accrington-Murphy armaments – are going to be sold to the warring factions in the forthcoming Jalapeno War. But where you are wrong is in assuming that I will make any profit from such transactions.'

'Sorry?' Blotto's brow furrowed. 'Not on the same page.'

'I have brought those fine Accrington-Murphy armaments into the country to help the starving children of Mexico.'

'How, by Denzil?' asked Blotto.

'I will give the armaments to the starving children of Mexico. They will sell them to the warring factions in the forthcoming Jalapeno War, in that way making enough money to buy food and stop starving.'

'Toad-in-the-hole, Syd!' said an admiring Blotto. 'You really are a Grade A foundation stone!'

Pollard smiled modestly. Just then their breakfasts arrived. While they ate, the tubby philanthropist talked more about his charity work.

And Blotto left, thinking soberly about how easy it could be to misjudge a boddo.

Sydney Pollard's thoughts were different. He was worried that the secret cache where he'd hidden the weapons had been found. That was dangerous information if it got spread around.

Sydney Pollard became determined to kill Blotto.

As he drove the Lagonda back to the Guiteras Ranch, Blotto reflected that he'd had a constructive morning. Snubbins to Twinks for suggesting he shouldn't do things off his own bat.

It didn't occur to him that his only real achievement had been to have increased the number of people who were determined to kill him.

11

Skulduggery in High Places

It might have been thought an act of aggression for El Chipito and his gang of desperados to appear at the Guiteras Ranch, but the meeting was by arrangement. General Henriquez Guiteras had invited them there. He wanted to hold high-level talks with the mercenary leader. Though he knew El Chipito was currently leaning towards the Partido Nacional Revolucionario faction, he also knew that he hadn't yet committed himself to that cause. And El Chipito had a long track record of changing sides.

So, while the supporting cast of desperados disported themselves in the ranch's various courtyards, drinking tequila, their boss was entertained with fine wine and finer cigars in their host's office.

'Obviously,' said the General, fastidiously favouring Spanish Spanish rather than the Mexican variety, 'you want more.'

'Obviously,' the mercenary agreed, in the local patois.

'More gold.'

'Precisely.'

'Well, that is exactly what I am offering you.'

'From where? You have to pay your forces too. Do you have a hidden supply of gold?'

'I do.' Hearing this, El Chipito smiled. 'The trouble is, it's currently also hidden from me.'

The smile left the mercenary's face. 'What do you mean?'

'I am referring to the Conquistadors' gold.'

'Ah. You are speaking of legends, folk stories, myths. I have heard people talking of the Conquistadors' gold since I was in the nursery, but nobody has got near to finding it.'

The General smiled. 'I have the means of finding it.'

An expression of cynicism put the straight line of El Chipito's scar out of true. 'Oh yes. You are not the first to have made that claim. Blah-blah, we all know the stories. The fine golden artefacts of the Aztecs were stolen and melted down by the Conquistadors, then hidden to be reclaimed and shipped back to Spain. That is one story. The other story is that the Conquistadors got the gold on to their ship, but it sank in the mid-Atlantic. Choose whichever version you like – no one has ever found the smallest grain of gold dust.'

'There is an English archaeologist called Professor Hector Troon-Wheatley. He knows more about Aztec civilisation than possibly anyone in the world.'

'What relevance has that? The story of the Conquistadors' gold has nothing to do with Aztec civilisation. If anything, it has to do with the Conquistadors' lack of civilisation.'

'Well, I believe Professor Hector Troon-Wheatley will discover the hidden gold. That is why I have given him licence to excavate the Attatotalloss Caves on my land. And when he finds that gold, El Chipito . . . half of it will be yours.'

'If, I presume, I take your side against the forces of the Partido Nacional Revolucionario . . . ?'

'Of course.'

The mercenary looked thoughtful. 'And what will happen to the English archaeologist? Isn't there a danger he might make some claim on the loot?'

'Once he has found the gold, he will, of course, be killed. I never waste time when it comes to killing people who get in my way.'

El Chipito nodded approvingly. He shared the same approach. 'Listen, General. I cannot be bought with fool's gold. If you find the real Conquistadors' gold, there is a very good chance I can be bought. But there is a deadline on this. The hidden treasure has not been found for four hundred years – why should it suddenly be found now?'

'Professor Hector Troon-Wheatley is an expert—'

'But, working on his own . . . I hear that his local workers have downed tools, because they claim to be afraid of the Curse of Attatotalloss. And if you believe that . . .'

'Do not worry,' said the General. 'I will see that he gets his workers back. And I will augment his strength with some of my own soldiers. With that amount of manpower, the Professor will have no difficulty finding the gold.'

'Huh.' The monosyllable was cynical. El Chipito didn't share the General's optimism. Still, he was prepared to continue their square dance of negotiation. 'Forty-eight hours,' he said. 'If I see the Conquistadors' gold with my own eyes within forty-eight hours, then maybe we can do business.'

'You mean you will then take my side against the forces of the Partido Nacional Revolucionario?'

'Possibly,' said El Chipito, with a scar-twitching smile. He hadn't built up his formidable reputation for always ending up on the right side by playing his cards too early.

'Good,' said General Henriquez Guiteras. 'I am confident we will have a deal.'

Both men took long swallows of their fine wine and longer puffs on their finer cigars. On El Chipito's side, there was an air of contentment. On the General's side, something more edgy.

After a silence, he said, 'There is, of course, something else I have to ask you . . .'

'Yes. What is it?' asked the mercenary innocently. Though he knew perfectly well what it was.

'Jalapeno City Jail.'

'Ah. Yes.'

'I had two prisoners incarcerated there, the Contreras father and son.'

'So I heard.'

'I assumed you would have done. You seem to know everything that happens in Jalapeno City.'

El Chipito nodded in silent acknowledgement of the compliment.

'Two nights ago, the prisoners were sprung from the Jalapeno City Jail.'

'I heard that too.'

'I thought, with the way you keep your ear to the ground in Jalapeno City, you might know the identity of the criminals who facilitated the escape.'

'It is, of course,' said El Chipito judiciously, 'possible that I might.'

'And also, that you might be able to tell me where General Ignacio Contreras and Carlos Contreras are now.'

The mercenary spread his hands wide in a gesture of helplessness as he told the blatant lie. 'I'm afraid I have no knowledge of their current whereabouts. I haven't seen either father or son since they went into prison.' In fact, he knew perfectly well that the two men had gone to the borders of Jalapeno, where the Partido Nacional Revolucionario forces were massing for their forthcoming onslaught.

General Henriquez Guiteras smiled graciously. 'Well, one cannot, of course, have everything. But the information about the identity of those who assisted the jail-breakers . . . you might be willing to share that with me . . . ?'

'Hmm . . .' The mercenary considered the proposition. 'I might. But if I were to give you that information, I might require an additional payment.'

'On top of half of the Conquistadors' gold?' asked the General, somewhat taken aback.

'Oh yes,' came the cool reply.

'What payment?'

'Your daughter Begonia.'

'You are asking to marry my daughter Begonia?'

'No, not marry.'

'Good.'

'Just have.'

'Ah.' It was General Henriquez Guiteras's turn to consider the proposition. He had absolutely no intention of handing over his precious daughter to be a mercenary's plaything. She was still destined to marry the man he had chosen for her, Colonel Alfredo Maldonado. In fact, the General thought, there might be arguments for speeding up that plan. If El Chipito had got his lustful eyes on Begonia . . . And if that young idiot Carlos Contreras was no longer in prison under sentence of death . . . And if war with the forces of the Partido Nacional Revolucionario was imminent . . .

Yes. General Henriquez Guiteras made the decision. His daughter's marriage to Colonel Alfredo Maldonado would take place the following day. He would see to it that the principals were informed of the change of plan.

But there was no need for El Chipito to know about it yet. Keep him in the dark a little longer, let him know about the wedding after it had happened, that was the best way. The General, like his mercenary adversary, didn't believe in playing his cards too early. 'Yes,' he said, in

113

response to El Chipito's request to 'have' his daughter. 'Of course. That would be quite acceptable . . .'

'Good.' The word was said with a satisfied smile.

'On the assumption, of course, that you tell me who sprung the two Contreras from Jalapeno City Jail.'

'Of course.' And El Chipito told him.

Though Blotto had had initial qualms about doing something that might discommode a person whose hospitality he was enjoying, the General had no such scruples about the idea of taking revenge on a house guest who he reckoned had done him wrong.

So, General Henriquez Guiteras's name was added to the list of people who wanted to kill Blotto.

The General's next action was to send a messenger to the gang-leader Refritos. He was to instruct his workforce to turn up at Professor Hector Troon-Wheatley's excavation site the following morning.

Blotto and Twinks were out riding, so plans for his execution were put on hold until their return. And, by the time they did get back, late that afternoon, there was a more pressing priority around the Guiteras Ranch.

Begonia had disappeared!

12

The Third Degree

If Blotto had hoped the panic prompted by the vanishing of Begonia would let him completely off the hook, he was due for disappointment. His plan, after a hot day's riding, had been a long soak in a bath with a couple of brandy and sodas to set him on the way for the evening's drinking. He was therefore not a little surprised to be snatched from his bedroom by armed guards before he'd had even the smallest slurp of B and S and marched off to the General's office.

Twinks, meanwhile, having heard the news of her friend's disappearance, had gone at once to Begonia's bedroom, the scene of many exchanged confidences between them. She was ready to use the full forensic kit which she carried in her sequined reticule to find clues as to what had happened to the girl, but she didn't need any of it. One look at Begonia's dressing table was enough to set her on the right track. One look in Begonia's wardrobe gave her all the further information she required.

And it wasn't very comforting.

* * *

Once inside the General's private domain, Blotto was further surprised to be treated by his host with positive hostility. The office was built on a gargantuan scale and every decoration, every weapon mounted on the wall, every framed citation, every draped flag, every bronze bust of himself on his desk was meant to be a testament to the power and military glory of General Henriquez Guiteras.

So did the new encrustations of golden epaulettes and tassels which had appeared on his white military jacket.

A sense of power seemed to emanate from his body as well, like an odour of unrestrained masculinity. His skin was very dark. He wore his hair long enough to look foppish on someone less threatening. It was an uncompromising black, as was the stubble which led the way into the thicket of his moustaches.

The General's English was good. His tone of voice wasn't. It was openly accusatory.

'So,' he said to Blotto, 'you have been springing prisoners out of Jalapeno City Jail.'

'Rein in the roans a moment there. I'd like to say—'

'Don't attempt to deny it!'

'I am not attempting to deny it, by Wilberforce! I'm just pointing out that those two poor greengages were only in Jalapeno City Jail because you had invented some leadpenny law to put them there.'

'You do not understand our Mexican legal system.'

'No, I do not.' Blotto was very honest. He didn't understand any legal system. 'But I can recognise when there's backdoor-sidling going on. And you'd lined the poor thimbles up for the firing squaddo. Introducing leadpenny laws simply to coffinate people is way beyond the barbed wire.'

'You are in no position to criticise me, Lord Lyminster. You are in no position to do anything. Illegally releasing convicted felons from prison is another offence which, here in Jalapeno Province, if nowhere else, merits the death penalty by firing squad.'

'Snubbins to you!' said Blotto, rather magnificently. 'You can do what you like to me. I will die, knowing that I have truth and justice on my side. Whereas you will never do anything without the knowledge that you're nothing more than a four-faced filcher!'

'Huh,' the General sneered. 'You are completely in my power, Lord Lyminster. Killing you would cause me no more reflection than killing a fly. But, before you face the firing squad, there is information you must give me.'

'I don't give any information to fumacious lumps of toadspawn,' said Blotto stoutly.

'You will,' said the General. 'And if you don't do so willingly, I have many means of persuasion at my command. My soldiers are highly trained in torture methods.' He relaxed into a smile. 'But, if you co-operate, Lord Lyminster, I will not have to resort to such barbarity. Simply tell me what I want to know, and you will be allowed to go free, with no more threats to your safety,' he lied. He had already decided that, for having contravened his newly invented law, Blotto would face the firing squad. He had decided when, too.

'Tell me what spoffing information you want then,' said Blotto. 'Come on, uncage the ferrets.'

'I want to know the present whereabouts of General Ignacio Contreras and his son Carlos. Where did you take them after you'd sprung them from Jalapeno City Jail?'

'I don't need to don my worry-boots about telling you that,' said Blotto. 'I handed them over straight from the prison, like loaves fresh out of the baking oven, to some thugbludgeon called El Chipotato—'

'El Chipito,' Guiteras suggested.

'That's the boddo! And he greeted them like a Buff Orpington greets a long-lost egg. A lot of clasping to bosoms went on which, I have to say, to my way of thinking, is way the wrong side of the running rail.'

'Never mind that. I don't believe you. El Chipito himself told me only hours ago that he had not seen either of the Contrerases.' But, even as he said the words, doubt crept insidiously into the General's mind. His knowledge of El Chipito's character should have stopped him from taking the man's words at face value so readily.

'Anyway, that is not important,' he said brusquely. 'There is other information I believe you are hiding from me, Lord Lyminster.'

'And what's that when it's got its spats on?'

'The whereabouts of my daughter Begonia.'

'About that, I'm afraid I haven't got a tinker's inkling.'

'Well, she's disappeared.'

'Yes. When I got back from riding, that bit of gin-gen stopped me in the stirrups. Well, that is to say, I was actually out of the stirrups when I heard the—'

The General cut through Blotto's waffle. 'But where is she? Where is my daughter?'

'I don't know a blind bezonger about that. But it might be something to do with "the truth of coarse love".'

'What?'

'Quote from an English writer-wallah known as Shakespeare. Don't know if you know the boddo ...?'

'Of course I have heard of Shakespeare.'

'Well, he penned a play about two young thimbles who wanted to twiddle the old reef-knot, but things kept getting in their way and they toddled through all kinds of gluepots. It's called *Rodeo and Juliet*.'

'*Romeo and Juliet*,' said the General instinctively.

'Good ticket. Anyway, in this play, the two young love-buds moon and mawk a lot and, basically, keep getting separated. And they expend a lot of sweat and swiggling to get back under the same umbrella. So . . .' Blotto smiled magnanimously, 'there is the answer to your questionette.'

'I don't know what you're talking about,' said General Henriquez Guiteras.

Blotto sighed heavily, as if having to explain a very simple concept to a particularly dense three-year-old. 'For Juliet, read your daughter Begonia. For Rodeo—'

'Romeo.'

'Good ticket. For that boddo, read Carlos Contreras. And there's the solutionette to your problemette.'

'Where?' asked a still-confused General.

Blotto sighed again. 'Your plumpilicious daughter, Begonia, has – clear as a kitten in a basket of puppies – gone to join her manly lovebud Carlos.'

'And where is he?'

'Are your lugs on the wonky? I just told you the whole clangdumble. Carlos Contreras and his father were last seen clasping bosoms with El Chipolata—'

'Chipito.'

'Good ticket.'

'And did my daughter tell you this was what she intended to do?'

'Not on your nuthatch. Shrimplets of a feminine per-suasion don't share that kind of guff with boddoes of a masculine persuasion. If they do uncage the ferrets on lovebuddery, they'd uncage them to another matching item of the gentler gender.'

Blotto realised his mistake as soon as he said it (a common failing with him, but he'd never been good at estimating the effect of his words before he uttered them).

'Aha!' General Henriquez Guiteras pounced on it. 'You are saying that my daughter confided in your sister, Lady Honoria?'

'No, no, not in a month of Thursdays,' Blotto protested.

But he was too late. General Henriquez Guiteras called out to an armed guard just outside the door, 'Bring Lady Honoria Lyminster to me!'

Twinks had had time to extricate herself from her riding gear and have a bath. She was now dressed in gossamer-thin silver evening wear. The perfume that emanated from her slender body diluted the stuffiness of the General's office.

'You are in serious trouble, Lady Lyminster,' he said, as soon as the guards brought her in.

'Oh, please call me "Twinks", General,' she said, with the smile whose swathe's efficiency in cutting through a generation of young men could only be compared to that of the Great War.

But General Henriquez Guiteras was not, at that moment, to be distracted. 'You are a close friend of my daughter Begonia,' he began. Then, he added, 'Twinks.' He rolled the word round his tongue like some culinary delicacy he'd just been asked to taste. His expression revealed that he didn't like it.

'Of course,' Twinks enthused. 'We're as close as two clams in the same chowder.'

'And so you exchange girlish secrets?'

'Of course,' Twinks assured him. 'And when we do, we're rolling on camomile lawns.'

'So . . . has Begonia told you where she has gone? Where she has disappeared to?'

Under their thick lashes, Twinks's azure eyes sought her brother's. They had not had a chance to communicate before their interrogations. She searched Blotto's face for some clue as to what he had told the General. As ever, his face remained blithely uncommunicative.

120

'I am sure, General,' she said, playing for time, 'that my bro has given you exactly the same spoffing gin-gen as I will.'

'Your brother has not held intimate conversations with my daughter.'

'No, but we think the same as two coddled eggs.' She looked again at Blotto. He smiled back at her, unhelpfully.

Fortunately, her interrogator himself helped her out. 'Lord Lyminster claims that my daughter has gone to be reunited with the unsuitable young man for whom she has formed a perverse attachment.'

'Yes,' said Blotto. 'Like in *Rodeo and Juliet*.'

'*Romeo*,' said Twinks and the General in unison.

Then the latter turned on the former. 'So, would you support what your brother told me? Did Begonia go to find the wretched Carlos Contreras?'

'Oh yes,' she agreed cheerily. 'Is the King German?'

The General looked puzzled. That particular rhetorical question didn't seem to have much traction in Mexico. He moved on. 'Did my daughter talk to you about her plans to meet up with this renegade?'

With hope, Twinks looked back again towards her brother. This time, she thought she detected the smallest inclination of his head. 'Oh yes,' she said. 'Begonia was very determined to find Carlos.'

'So, you helped her?'

'Doesn't one always want to help young lovebuds? One wants their life to be all creamy éclair.' She spoke with a winsomeness which had a track record for melting the most permafrosted of masculine hearts.

It didn't work with General Henriquez Guiteras, though. His brow loured like a thunderstorm as he boomed, 'And if you, Lady Lyminster, helped my daughter go to meet her contemptible lover, you no doubt also helped him escape from Jalapeno City Jail.'

121

Blotto intervened on his sister's behalf. 'No, fair biddles. Twinks didn't have a salami's part in the actual springing of the boddoes from the jail.'

'Ah.' The General's expression looked a little conciliatory.

And then Blotto went and spoiled things by saying cheerily, 'No, her only contrib to the party was planning the whole clangdumble.'

'Guards!' General Henriquez Guiteras roared, reverting to his rather fastidious Spanish (which, of course, Twinks understood perfectly). 'Imprison these two!'

There were six guards and a slight shake of the head from his sister stopped Blotto from attempting to resist them. Besides, he hadn't got his cricket bat with him.

'Take them to Jalapeno City Jail, General?' asked the chief guard.

'No. Imprison them here. Jalapeno City Jail's walls have proved to be rather porous recently. These two are not going to escape.'

'Very good, General. We take them to the lockup by the stables.'

'No. The dungeon!'

The expression on the guard's face showed how unusual this instruction was. It was also a measure of the seriousness of the prisoners' crimes.

'There they will await trial . . . for offences committed in contravention of the laws which I have just had passed.'

The two siblings exchanged looks. Twinks – and even Blotto – knew the penalty for transgressing the General's new laws.

And the guards smiled wolfishly. They enjoyed the shooting gallery attraction of firing squads.

The dungeon was only partly man-made. Its walls, unsteadily lit by flickering wall-mounted torches, showed natural rock as well as brickwork. So there had been caves under this part of the Guiteras mansion. On arrival, Twinks idly speculated about the possibility of there being an underground link to the site of Troon-Wheatley's excavation. But it seemed unlikely. Too neat. And the distance was too great. The bubble idea of making an escape by that route quickly burst.

Blotto didn't share his sister's thoughts. He wasn't much given to speculation, idle or otherwise. But he did share Twinks's desire to extricate themselves from their current gluepot. He wasn't cast down, though. Prisons didn't dispirit him. He'd escaped from so many over the years, he regarded them just as an occupational hazard for any young boddo to whom danger seemed to cling like an unwanted corn plaster. He only wished he had his cricket bat with him.

He didn't make any suggestions as to how they should escape. He felt confident Twinks would have some ideas. And she was bound to have some useful jail-breaking equipment in her sequined reticule. She always had.

But when she started talking to him, it wasn't about escape.

'So, Blotters, you reckon that what the General was gabbing about unscrews the corkscrew, do you?'

'Sorry, sis. Not on the same page?'

'You reckon it's lovebuddery? That Begonia has gone off to moon and mawk with her tasty slice of redcurrant cheesecake?'

'Seems the right size of pyjamas. Like Rodeo and—'

'Romeo,' said Twinks.

'Good ticket. And you said that's what you and Begonia chewed the breeze about.'

'Yes, but I wasn't delivering the right goods. Beggers and I didn't have any whiffle-whaffle about her going off to join Carlos.'

'Didn't you, by Denzil?'

'No, I only agreed with the General because I thought that was the fly you'd flicked in his direction. I thought you had a stratagemette to feed him that particular spaghetti.'

'Me? Have a stratagemette?' asked a bewildered Blotto.

'No. Probably not,' his sister agreed. But there had to be a first time for everything.

'So, if you don't think Begonia's playing chumbos with Carlos, what in the name of strawberries do you think she is doing?'

'I think she's been abducted,' said Twinks.

'Abducted? What got that thought stirring among the grey cells?'

'I went to Begger's bedroom when we got back from our horse-hacking. And I checked the poor little thimble's wardrobe.'

'Sorry? Not on the same page?'

'I know all Begonia's toggings from tiara to toe-strap. And all of the shimmeries were there except for her cotton day dress. Doesn't that set your braincells blipping?'

'No,' Blotto replied, with complete honesty.

'What it means, brother of mine, is that Begonia did not leave the ranch of her own accord.'

'Still not on the same bus, sister of mine.'

'Listen, Blotters, if we assumed the view that you rather cleverly shuffled past the General ...' Blotto smiled modestly – it wasn't often that his name and the expression 'rather cleverly' were used in the same sentence. '... that Begonia packed her tents to go and meet her special piece of raspberry cheesecake – i.e. Carlos Contreras – then there's not an ice-cube's chance in a furnace she'd have left wearing a cotton day dress. She'd have biddled herself up a bit. It's one of the first rules for a love-languisher.'

'Good ticket,' said Blotto, not for the first time confused by the priorities of the gentler gender.

'And,' Twinks continued, 'as if that wasn't the full load of fish, the poor little greengage had left her handbag on the dressing table. So, you know what that means, don't you?'

'No,' said Blotto, again scrupulously honest.

'It means that Begonia didn't leave the Guiteras Ranch voluntarily. As I spelled out in six-footers just now, she was abducted.'

'But who'd want to abduct an eye-wobbler like Begonia?'

'Any number of four-faced filchers. Slugbuckets who want to use her as a bargaining counter with her father. Boddoes after a spoffing ransom payment. Stenchers who fancy having a breath-sapper like Begonia in their harems. You name it, there's some lump of toadspawn out there ready to try it on.'

'Then, by Wilberforce,' Blotto asserted, 'we must rescue her!'

'Bingbopper of an idea, Blotto me old washboard,' said Twinks. 'But rescuing the poor little thimble from inside the guts of this prison is going to be a tough rusk to chew.'

'Surely you've got something in your sequined reticule that will help us to break out?'

Twinks shook her head.

'But you have got a planette to turn everything back to creamy éclair, haven't you?' said Blotto confidently.

'No,' said Twinks, sinking to sit on the prison floor. 'I haven't.'

Blotto looked bewildered. For his sister not to have a planette really was the flea's armpit.

'Broken biscuits,' he murmured. Once again, the situation really was that bad.

*   *   *

125

He didn't actually know how bad it was. But Twinks did. Blotto, having no language skills, didn't know what the guards had said as they thrust the two prisoners into the dungeon and slammed the metal doors closed on them.

Twinks, though, had understood their dialogue perfectly.

'Do you think the General will put them on trial tomorrow morning?' asked the first guard.

'No,' the second replied. 'I think he is getting bored with the whole process of trials. They cause an unnecessary delay in the legal process.'

'Yes,' said the first with relish. 'If I know the General, he will follow the procedure he did with that peon who insulted him the day before yesterday.'

'You mean . . . ?'

'Yes. No faffing around with a trial. Straight to the firing squad.'

'So, when do you reckon he'd have that planned for with these two?'

'Tomorrow morning. At dawn.' The first guard chuckled. He enjoyed being part of a firing squad. Good target practice.

No wonder Twinks wore the expression of someone in whose custard a large number of lumps had just appeared.

13

Corky's Complications

Corky Froggett liked to keep life simple. He had had the great good fortune to enjoy the intimate company of a surprising number of women. Though a mere serf in the eyes of the aristocrats he served (with the exception of Blotto and Twinks, and their empathy with him could vanish on certain social occasions), he had more of a profile below stairs. There, being a chauffeur carried some clout. The fact that he had a black uniform with shiny buttons and a peaked cap contributed to his appeal. And his knowledge of the workings of the (still relatively new) internal combustion engine also set him on something of a pedestal. Such things counted in the world of cooks, kitchen maids and chambermaids.

None of Corky's skirmishes with the gentler gender had caused his ramrod demeanour to bend much. Though appreciative of the woman he was sharing an umbrella with at any given moment, parting from her caused him few qualms. He had found that, in common with buses, there'd be another one along in a minute.

It should not be assumed by anyone unacquainted with the life story of Corky Froggett that his horny hide had never been penetrated by Cupid's arrows. During what he still referred to as 'the recent little dust-up in France', he had made the acquaintance of a daring undercover fighter called Yvette. And she had prompted in his manly breast feelings he had never before encountered.

Sadly, they were parted by the fortunes of war, but fate reunited them some years later, when Yvette was operating as a couturier in London, under the soubriquet of Madame Clothilde of Mayfair. Love blossomed again, though sadly it was cut short when Corky thought that his romantic obsession had got in the way of his primary duty, ensuring the safety of the young master, Blotto.

That experience had built Corky Froggett a carapace against the deeper passions, and he had subsequently made do with a sequence of charming second bests. (Though he had had the tact never to mention to any of them that they were second best.)

The main rule he followed in his love-life was: Keep it simple. One relationship at a time. And there were two signs which told him when it was the moment to move on. First, when a woman became clingy and started talking about a future together. And, second, when a woman became jealous.

Unfortunately, Carmelita had recently started flagging up the second sign. The affair had started well. The chauffeur's uniform had proved as attractive a lure in Mexico as it had in the Land of Golden Lions. And the convenience of Carmelita's fairy grotto, with its pervasive odour of refried beans, had been fully taken advantage of.

Corky had initially mispronounced her name as 'Carnalita' and, to his considerable satisfaction, this had proved apposite. Their encounters also benefited from her busy work schedule, which meant they couldn't last long and didn't leave much time for conversation. Which, given their mutual ignorance of each other's language, was probably just as well.

The rift that came between them had arisen from a misunderstanding. The afternoon when Blotto and Twinks returned from riding to face the wrath of General Henriquez Guiteras, reaching under the chassis to remove an intransigent speck of dust from the Lagonda's wheel bearings, Corky had inadvertently snagged his uniform jacket on the edge of the car's secret compartment. His moving away had sheared off one of the polished brass buttons and he had gone into the kitchen to find Carmelita with a view to her sewing it back on for him.

Sadly, when he arrived, she was off on a chore, collecting cheese from the dairy. So, Corky had jovially asked if any of the other kitchen staff could sort out his predicament.

It was unfortunate that Lucia, the chambermaid who volunteered to take on the task, had a history of bad blood with Carmelita. A few months earlier, both had had their eyes on the same stable lad and, though Carmelita's superior seduction technique had won the day, the victory still rankled with her rival.

It was also unfortunate that, at the time Corky entered the kitchen, having left his boots in the fairy grotto, Lucia was the only other person present. Helpfully, she had removed his jacket to perform her act of needlework rescue and, equally helpfully, she had suggested that, since they were sitting so near the kitchen range, he might be more comfortable if he removed his undershirt. And, because of the heat, she, perfectly reasonably, had loosened her blouse too.

That was the explanation Corky Froggett gave for the scene Carmelita encountered on her return from the dairy. Given the past history between the two women, she didn't believe a word of it. And she wasn't reticent in telling him why she didn't believe it.

Though the chauffeur had no Spanish, there are times when language is not needed for an understanding of what someone is saying. It happens when two people are in love. It also happens when two people are in hate. This was one of the second occasions. And, once Carmelita's diatribe had started, she showed no signs of wanting to stop it.

For their relationship, the writing was very definitely on the wall. Corky would happily have ended the affair there and then, but there was a snag. Assuming a continuity of their cohabitation, he had moved all of his belongings into Carmelita's fairy grotto. And, once she had wrung her lungs out shouting at him, she had announced that she was unwell and retired to bed for the rest of the evening.

Corky knew that going straight to her sleeping quarters to reclaim his possessions would only trigger more vituperation. So, he decided to wait until she had cried herself to sleep, before slipping into the fairy grotto and silently extracting his stuff. Then, the following day, he might explore the possibility of getting closer to Lucia. He wondered whether she, too, had a convenient fairy grotto somewhere.

To kill time, he went round the mansion, looking for the young master and the young mistress, but could find no sign of them. He assumed they were still out riding.

It was not in Twinks's nature to be cast down for long. And Blotto's interpretation of her behaviour when they were first thrust into the dungeon – that she had given up hope – was wrong. Sure, she had been knocked back by what she had heard the guards say, and the realisation of how short the window was for them to escape.

But all she'd said to Blotto was that she hadn't got a planette. What she meant was that she hadn't got a planette *yet*.

Very quickly she was up again, both physically and mentally. Augmenting the flickering light from the flaming torches with that from the electric one out of her sequined reticule, she was soon examining the walls, floor and ceiling of their jailhouse.

'It'll be larksissimo, Blotters me old spud-scraper,' she said, 'when we get out of here.'

'Good ticket,' he agreed enthusiastically. 'We'll be rolling on camomile lawns.'

But his sister's reconnaissance of the space didn't offer any immediate escape opportunities. The doors through which they had been thrust were thick metal, with double locks and steel bars slotted across on the other side. The prison's floor and ceiling were solid natural rock. So were most of the walls, though the two ends of the original cave had been bricked off to make an almost rectangular space.

And the brickwork was recent, not featuring the kind of crumbling mortar that could be conveniently picked away at with a nail file from the sequined reticule . . . as happened in so many daring escape stories.

Twinks detected the slightest of breezes on her face. But its source wasn't the hidden door which could be conveniently prised open in the same daring escape stories. The breath of air came from two narrow ventilation pipes set inaccessibly high in one of the brick walls. Presumably, whoever had designed the jail had not wanted its inmates to die of asphyxiation. That would spoil the fun of the firing squad.

Twinks didn't express to her brother the frustration caused by this lack of obvious escape route. She checked the silver pocket watch in her sequined reticule. Six hours to dawn.

And she knew all too well what was due to happen then.

'Dammit!'

It was his shaving mug. Corky Froggett had been so

careful. He had lurked outside Carmelita's fairy grotto until he had heard her cry herself to sleep, her reproachful sobbing melting gradually into a sighing slumber. Then he had given it half an hour before approaching the cave entrance in stockinged feet. (This wasn't difficult because his boots were among the possessions that still had to be rescued from Carmelita's domain.)

The operation tested every aspect of his military training, and he applied the skills he'd acquired during 'the last little dust-up in France'. Creeping up behind enemy sentries to garotte them had taught him how to move in total silence. Preparation for night manoeuvres had got him into the habit of memorising every detail of a landscape which he might next encounter after dark.

So, as he entered Carmelita's fairy grotto, he knew exactly where he had left his spare shirts and underwear, the canvas knapsack containing his toothbrush and shaving kit and – most importantly – his boots.

Inching his way into the darkness, his hands found all his possessions exactly where he had remembered leaving them. He loaded his arms with them, listening to Carmelita's even breathing, and was about to leave as silently as he had arrived. When he remembered his shaving mug. And he remembered that he'd left it, after shaving that morning, on Carmelita's bedside table.

Corky Froggett was not a sentimental man. His iron military discipline had long ago strained any softer feelings out of him. Except for his loyalty to the Lyminster family – and particularly the young master – which was undying (or, preferably, dying in their service), he did not indulge the softer emotions.

But there was a space in his heart for the shaving mug. An example of rustic Breton ceramics, it had been given to him by Yvette (a.k.a. Madame Clothilde of Mayfair). To lose it would be an insult to the sanctity of that great love.

Though the cave's interior was pitch black, Corky knew exactly where on the bedside table he had left the mug. He could virtually see the thing as his hand moved forward to pick it up.

But he had not considered the possibility of its having been moved by Carmelita. Comfort-eating to heal her cheated heart, she craved refried beans. And in placing her bowl of them on the bedside table, she had moved the shaving mug. No more than six inches nearer the table edge than it had been left, but enough of a change of position for Corky's hand to brush against the mug and send it flying to shatter on the cave's stone floor.

It was that crash which had prompted his 'Dammit!'

Worse than that, though, it had also prompted a scream from Carmelita, frightened at the abrupt ending of her sleep. Knowing instinctively who the intruder was, her scream was quickly followed by the resumption of her denunciation of men in general and Corky Froggett in particular.

Another lesson from his wartime experiences was to recognise the moment when it was time to retreat. He recognised it and made for the exit.

But he hadn't planned for an assault from a furious, vituperative Mexican woman who snatched his boots from him and flung them to the furthest recesses of her cave.

'You little vixen!' shouted Corky. 'I'll have your guts for garters!'

'I'll have your guts for garters,' Twinks echoed.

'I beg your parsnips,' said Blotto. 'Not on the same page?'

'I just heard a voice I recognise say, "I'll have your guts for garters."'

'A voice you recognise? Was it saying the gutty stuff in Spanish?'

'No, of course it wasn't, Blotto me old soft pedal. It was in English.'

Her brother looked puzzled. 'Well, who do we spoffing well know in Jalapeno who might—?'

He was interrupted by a shout of, 'Don't you dare put refried beans in my boots!' In the unmistakable tones of his chauffeur, Corky Froggett.

Twinks had quickly identified that the sound was coming through the ventilation pipes. By some bizarre coincidence, Corky Froggett seemed to have materialised on the other side of the brick wall.

It took a while to attract his attention. However much Blotto and Twinks shouted, they were outshouted by a furious Carmelita, possibly still gaining her revenge on the chauffeur's perfidy by filling his boots with more refried beans.

Eventually, though, as all storms must, hers subsided, awaiting a second wind. And into that merciful silence was inserted a cry from Twinks: 'Corky, for the love of strawberries, get us out of this treacle tin!'

This time, the chauffeur definitely heard Twinks. 'It's amazing,' his responding voice trickled through the ventilation pipes. 'I'll swear that was the young mistress.'

How she had heard it, having learned no English at school and having heard little of it in Jalapeno Province, but somehow Carmelita did understand the word 'mistress'. And she definitely took it the wrong way. 'So, Corky, you have another mistress!' she bawled and resumed her diatribe.

It took a while to get the facts sorted. Had the ventilation pipes not been so high up the wall, communication would have been easier, but after much shouting and misunderstanding, Corky Froggett understood the basics. Blotto and Twinks were incarcerated in an underground prison which turned out to be part of the same cave system as Carmelita's fairy grotto. A solid brick wall had been erected between the two spaces.

Twinks issued instructions as to what Corky should do about this regrettable situation. He should fetch the Lagonda and park it as near as possible to the entrance to Carmelita's premises. He should then get out the required pickaxes and shovels from the luggage compartment. Once he had made a hole big enough to pass a pickaxe through, Blotto would take it and, working from both sides, the two of them should quickly demolish enough of the wall for the prisoners to escape.

Oh, and Twinks casually remarked, there was an element of urgency about the scenario. She and Blotto were due to be shot by a firing squad at dawn.

As was so often the case, everything went as Twinks had planned it.

She had initially worried that the noise of demolition might attract unwanted attention from General Henriquez Guiteras's guards. But no problem arose. The ranch's customary late-night carousing made a hell of a racket. And Carmelita did not allow the destruction of her fairy grotto to deflect her from continuing to excoriate Corky Froggett and wishing all kinds of perdition on the faithless Lucia.

Her unending litany of curses drowned out the sound of the pickaxes. Hearing her, the Guiteras guards thought nothing of it. Carmelita had always conducted the ups and downs of her love-life in a rather public manner.

It was an hour before dawn when the Lagonda left the Guiteras Ranch, hopefully for the last time. It was a relief for Corky finally to hear the screaming invective of Carmelita fade into the distance. Though he couldn't understand any of the individual words, he got a pretty good sense of their meaning. (Had he asked Twinks, which he didn't, she would have told him that the kitchen maid was raining curses on him and his family, including those who were dead and those who were not yet born. And Carmelita was assuring him that she would get her revenge one day. No one treated her as he had and got away with it.)

As he drove out through the main gates, Blotto let out a cry of 'Toad-in-the-hole!'

Twinks shared his ecstatic mood with a cry of 'Larksissimo!' Then she added, 'Now, we go and find Begonia!'

Corky Froggett was silent. He was sad to have seen the last of the Breton shaving mug he'd been given by Yvette.

Also, it would affect the dignity of any chauffeur to have his black leather boots filled with refried beans.

14

In Search of Begonia

'Do you think, sister of mine,' asked Blotto, 'that once the stenchers have realised we've scuttled down the drainpipe, they'll go into full bloodhound to recapture us?'

'I think, thank Disraeli, they won't, brother of mine. They've got bigger racks of ribs on their plate. The conflict's blue touchpaper will be lit very soon. The Partido Nacional Revolucionario forces are massing on the borders of Jalapeno Province. The Guiteras supporters'll fix the focus on them rather than us.'

'So, nothing will stop us from springing Begonia out of her clinkbox?'

'Well, there is the small matter of finding her. But that'll be as easy as a one-bush maze, so everything will soon be creamy éclair.'

'Hoopee-doopee!' said Blotto.

Corky Froggett continued to wonder when they would stop long enough for him to empty his boots. The possibility of spilling refried beans in the interior of the Lagonda went against everything he held sacred.

With the approach of the long-anticipated war between the

Partido Nacional Revolucionario and General Henriquez Guiteras's rebels, Sydney Pollard had moved into action. Being a gun-runner of great fairness, he had divided the cache of weapons in Professor Hector Troon-Wheatley's excavation site exactly in two. One half of the armoury he had sent to the government forces, and the other half to the General. Both had been delivered by Kelrilos's mule cart. And the gang-leader had added a supply of his custom-made hand-grenades, for the appropriate remuneration, to each order.

It was only a matter of time before the bloody conflict began. General Henriquez Guiteras, along with Colonel Pedro Jiminez and his other acolytes started to muster their private armies.

As usual, Twinks was very clear about their plan of action. Though she had listed the kind of people who might have abducted Begonia, she didn't relish getting involved in random searching. She wanted specific information to lead them to their quarry and she felt confident that she would find it at the Cactus Flower Hotel in Jalapeno City. If she drew blanks there, she would consult Diego the café proprietor.

Blotto and Corky Froggett, both unquestioning, followed her lead. Blotto, secure in the knowledge that his cricket bat was in the back of the Lagonda, was excited at the prospect of action. His chauffeur would still have felt more comfortable if he'd had an opportunity to empty his boots of refried beans.

The first person Twinks sought out at the Cactus Flower Hotel was Sydney Pollard. She thought, quite correctly, that he was in touch with most of the likely participants in the forthcoming war and he kept his ear very close to the ground. If there were rumours to be heard, Sydney Pollard would hear them.

They were lucky to catch him. The tubby little man, the inevitable cigar between his lips, was standing in the hotel foyer in front of a considerable pile of luggage. He did not need to explain that he was on his way out of Jalapeno City. As soon as the mule-cart he'd ordered arrived.

'Pongling off now?' asked a surprised Blotto. 'Just when the balloon's tearing free of its spoffing guy-ropes.'

'I do not like war,' said the gun-runner. 'It upsets my digestion.'

'That's a bit of a rum baba,' said Twinks. 'Given that your jobbo is providing boddoes in wartime with the means to coffinate each other.'

Sydney Pollard raised an admonitory finger. 'No, that is not my business,' he said. 'All I do is supply people with armaments. What they do with those armaments is up to them.'

'I don't know how you can have the brass front to say that.' Blotto was still smarting from the way he'd been duped into assisting Pollard's gun-running. 'You're a spoffing hippodrome!'

'Hypocrite,' said Twinks gently.

'That too,' her brother agreed.

'Anyway, no time to fritter,' said Twinks. 'Before you scuttle off like a rat down the mooring rope, I need some information from you.'

'And what makes you think that I have any information I want to share with you?'

'What makes me spoffing well think that,' said Twinks with a steely edge, 'is that if you don't share it, my brother and our chauffeur would think it was pure creamy éclair to detach your limbs from your torso.'

The use of violent threats, except in case of self-defence,

139

was not something Twinks usually condoned. But, for a gun-runner, she was prepared to make an exception.

The expression on Sydney Pollard's face suggested he thought she was serious, and he hastily said, 'What information do you require?'

'You will have received the gin-gen that Begonia Guileras has been abducted?' said Twinks. Pollard nodded. 'We need to know what four-faced filcher has abducted her.'

The tubby man looked distressed. 'I don't know anything about that,' he said.

'Yes, you do, by Wilberforce.'

'No, I don't, I—'

'Do you want me to uncage my brother with his cricket bat on you?'

Twinks sounded very threatening. And, being English, Sydney Pollard knew the destruction that could be wreaked by a cricket bat in the right hands.

'All right, all right!' He held up his hands in concession.

And he gave them the information.

The moment he'd given it, a peon came into the hotel foyer to tell him that his mule-cart had arrived.

So, the gun-runner and the group from Tawcester Towers parted company, with fervent hopes on both sides that their paths would never cross again. And Sydney Pollard went off in search of the next 'international incident'.

Twinks hadn't been surprised by the destination Sydney Pollard had suggested. If she had just been guessing, the Lazy Iguana Ranch would have been near the top of her list. She had quickly identified the jealousy in the personality of Colonel Pedro Jiminez. Though sycophantic to the point of toadyism in the company of General

Henriquez Guiteras, the younger man was permanently conscious of the ways in which he failed to measure up to his superior. His rank was junior, his ranch was smaller and, despite all his braggadocio, he was less successful with women. Everything about him was inferior. And that was a source of constant discomfort to him.

Kidnapping his rival's daughter might just be a petulant way of getting back at him. Alternatively, there could be some more elaborate plan behind the abduction. Twinks didn't get the impression that Jiminez's loyalty to his boss was of the most durable kind.

When they arrived at the Lazy Iguana Ranch, the scenario did not seem as bad as it might have been. Colonel Pedro Jiminez seemed actually to be waiting for them. But, remarkably, with no evil intent.

They had parked the Lagonda outside the main gates. Corky Froggett had been instructed to stay with the car unless summoned. And, as Blotto and Twinks entered the heavily guarded compound, the Colonel came striding towards them, his face wreathed in smiles (as well as black moustaches).

Twinks was prepared for more of Jiminez's fatuous assertions of his love for and determination to marry her, but he offered no such overtures.

'Welcome!' he cried. 'I have been expecting you.'

'Oh? What?' asked Twinks, not letting her protective *froideur* get any less *froid*.

'Because,' the Colonel replied, 'I had been expecting that you would come in search of Begonia Guiteras.'

'So, you are not denying that you're keeping her in a clinkbox here?'

'Hardly that,' came the disingenuous reply. 'I am holding Begonia here for her own safety . . . Twinks.'

141

She didn't argue with his use of the name, but she did say, 'Oh yes? And if you think I'm going to believe that, then I'm an Apache dancer!'

'What I say is true,' protested Jiminez, as if grievously misunderstood. 'If you do not believe me, go and ask Begonia herself.'

'Where is she?' Twinks demanded.

The Colonel pointed. 'Go along that corridor, past the orange blossom, turn right at the wrought-iron gate, and you will find your friend sitting in the garden there.'

Without a word Twinks hurried off, following the directions she had been given.

Blotto grinned at Colonel Pedro Jiminez and tried to think of something to say to him. Their previous encounter had been brief, when he had come to rescue his sister from near the iguana enclosure. And then he recalled wanting to batter the oikish sponge-worm from the Oval to Lord's via Edgbaston. Not much basis for an easy ongoing conversation.

Blotto decided to play it safe and asked, 'Do you play cricket at all?'

'No,' replied the Colonel.

'Fair biddles,' said Blotto, and tried to think of something to add. 'When it comes to conversation,' he went on, grasping at straws, 'I'm afraid I'm a bit of an empty revolver.'

'That is not important,' said Jiminez.

'No, I suppose it spoffing well isn't,' Blotto agreed. Then, 'You can say that with two cherries on.'

Another silence. Then, that rare bird of passage, a thought, came into his head. 'When, just now, you gabbed that you were holding that little shrimplet Begonia "for her own safety", what was your meaningette?'

'I meant,' the Colonel replied, 'that the girl was in danger at the Guiteras Ranch.'

'In spoffing danger? What, with her own Pater?'

'She is in no direct danger from her father. He will not harm her. But his actions might put her in danger.'

'How? Sorry, not reading your semaphore.'

'You know there is soon to be armed conflict between the Mexican government and General Henriquez Guiteras?'

'Ah yes. Something of that order did blip on the brain-cells. In fact, everyone keeps replaying the same cylinder on the subject.'

'As you may know, I've always been on the General's side . . . ?'

'No, that hadn't clicked the clocker.'

'Well, I have been. And I'm on his side partly because he looked likely to win. His forces are well-trained. The government have got a ragbag of peons and ne'er-do-wells for an army.'

'Have they, by Denzil?'

'They have. Or, rather, they had. But recently they've been put under the generalship of a mercenary leader called El Chipito.'

'I've heard of the boddo,' said Blotto, with something like triumph.

'El Chipito's really licking the layabouts into shape. The government's always had greater numbers than General Guiteras. Now they've got better military expertise too. So, as to which side I support, I'm considering my position.'

'But surely,' said Blotto, 'you wouldn't think of playing a diddler's hand with your old chumbo, would you?'

'Why not?' The Colonel spoke as if the question had never occurred to him.

'Well, I mean,' Blotto expostulated, 'ratting on a chumbo is way the wrong side of the barbed wire. It goes against every principle of truth and justice. It's not the British way.'

'So?' Colonel Pedro Jiminez shrugged. 'I am not British. Anyway,' he went on, 'I and a few other of Guiteras's long-time allies are thinking twice about supporting him. Without us, he'll definitely be defeated. Which is why I have taken charge of the General's daughter, Begonia. For her own safety.'

'What, so . . .' As ever, Blotto pieced things together slowly '. . . if her Pater gets boffed by El Chipito and his pistol-packers, Begonia's Stilton will be distinctly iffy.'

'Exactly. I happen to know that El Chipito has his eyes on the girl. He wants her to be part of his harem.' Responding to a look of puzzlement on Blotto's face, 'You know what a harem is?'

Blotto was about to reply honestly that he had no idea, when a memory came back to him of something one of the Classics beaks at Eton had told him. 'Is it a Roman war galley with three banks of oars?' he suggested hopefully.

'No,' the Colonel replied. 'That is a trireme.'

'Good ticket.'

'A harem is where Muslim men lock up their women-folk.'

'What for?' asked Blotto.

'So that they are readily available.'

'What for?' asked Blotto.

But Jiminez had done enough explaining. 'So, I have rescued Begonia Guiteras from the evil clutches of El Chipito.'

'Well then, you're on the right side of right. I know I may have said that your ratting on your chumbos was outside the rule book, but your rescuing that little shrimplet puts a lot of tonnage into the other scale. You're made of pure brick-mix, Colonel. In fact, not to fiddle round the fir trees, Colonel, you're a Grade A foundation stone!'

'Thank you, Lord Lyminster.'

'Blotto, please.'

'Thank you then, Blotto.'

'No skin off my rice pudding.'

'But,' said the Colonel earnestly, 'I am still worried for Begonia Guiteras's safety, even here at the Lazy Iguana Ranch.'

'Oh? Why's that?'

'Warfare is dangerous. The innocent can get caught in the crossfire . . .'

'You're bong on the nose there.'

'. . . which is why I am so pleased that you and your sister have arrived.'

'Oh?'

'I was hoping you could take Begonia away to a place of greater safety.'

'Buzzbanger of an idea!' Blotto enthused.

'Then let us do it straight away. The sooner, the better. I will fetch the two young ladies. You go out to your splendid car and get her started. Then you can drive off and I need never worry about Begonia Guiteras's safety again.'

'Hoopee-doopee!' said Blotto.

Colonel Pedro Jiminez went back towards his house and Blotto joined Corky Froggett in the Lagonda. He didn't notice how much more relaxed the chauffeur looked than when they had parted. Much more comfortable since he had managed to empty his boots of refried beans.

'Spoffing amazing,' said Blotto to Corky, as he settled in the passenger seat, 'how a boddo can get a boddo wrong. I had thought, when I first met that Jiminez greengage, that he was a total lump of toadspawn, but when I get to know him better, he turns out to be totally on the good side of the egg basket.'

Blotto might have continued expatiating for some time on the basic decency of the Colonel and what a lot he was doing to take care of Begonia, had they not heard the heavy sound of the huge main gates being closed and locked.

Blotto realised, slowly, that he had been duped. Not only was Begonia Guiteras a prisoner in the Lazy Iguana Ranch. Now Twinks was too.

15

Action Stations!

Blotto was shocked as Corky Froggett suddenly pressed the self-starter and urged the great car forward. 'Rein in the roans a moment there!' he cried. 'My sister's inside that spoffing place! I'm going to rescue the little shrimplet – and her chumbo Begonia! Lyminsters don't turn their backs on the four-faced filchers who do them wrong! Stop the car!'

For possibly the first time in their relationship, the chauffeur ignored one of the young master's commands and drove on.

'Why, in the name of Wilberforce, aren't you stopping, Corky?'

'Look at the tops of the walls, milord.'

Blotto screwed his head round to see the compound's wall crested by Jiminez's desperados. All with rifles, all firing in their direction.

'I'm not afraid of bullets from that load of limp-rags,' Blotto insisted. 'They've got Twinks, but I've got my cricket bat. And my strength is as the strength of ten because my heart is pure. Turn the car round, Corky!'

'No, milord,' said the chauffeur, the first time he'd

ever responded that way to an order from the young master.

'Why not, in the name of ginger?' demanded Blotto, uncharacteristically furious.

'Because, milord,' Corky Froggett replied humbly, 'suppose one of their bullets pierced the bodywork of the Lagonda?'

'Ah,' said Blotto, immediately pacified. 'I read your semaphore. Can't risk that, can we?'

'No, milord.'

'Savvy thinking, Corky. We'll find another way to get Twinks out of the clinkbox.'

And the Lagonda drove on across the plains of Mexico.

This was one of those moments when Blotto would have given a lot to have Twinks beside him. Not only because he didn't like to think of her in the clutches of a desperado like Colonel Pedro Jiminez, but also because he hadn't a clue as to what he should do next. And his sister certainly would have.

'I say, Corky me old rind-remover, you wouldn't have an idea of how we get Twinks out of her current gluepot?'

'By rescuing her, milord.'

'Good ticket. But how do we rescue her?'

'Ah. That I don't know, milord.'

'Well, what do you reckon we need, Corky, except having Twinks here to give us some beezer wheeze?'

Remembering what he'd learned about military planning during the last little dust-up in France, the chauffeur replied, 'We need information, milord. Do you know anywhere where we can get information?'

'Do you know,' said Blotto, a relieved smile playing around his lips, 'I think I do.'

* * *

'I remember,' said Isadora del Plato. 'And I meant what I said. To you, Blotto, I would give information for free. And do you know why?'

'Not in a year of Februarys.'

'I would give you anything for free,' she breathed, 'because you are one of the best-looking men I have ever met.'

Blotto blushed to the roots of his hair. 'Don't talk such toffee,' he said.

If Isadora del Plato had hoped that her avowal might have led to some action on his part, she quickly swallowed her disappointment and asked, 'So, Blotto, what kind of information can I give you?'

He quickly explained about the abduction of Begonia Guiteras and his sister's incarceration with her in the Lazy Iguana Ranch. 'And I was wondering whether, amongst all this information you seem to have spilling out of your sugar sacks, you might know a secret way my chauffeur and I could get inside the fumacious place and winkle the little droplets out.'

Isadora del Plato gave him the relevant instructions.

El Falleza once again saw Blotto leaving the room of his inamorata. If his loathed rival hadn't called down the stairs to his chauffeur, the bullfighter would have attacked him there and then. The sword with which he had ended the life of so many magnificent *toros* was sharpened and ready.

El Falleza realised he would have to wait, and seethed quietly.

Willy 'Ruffo' Walberswick hadn't lost touch with the flame-haired Estrella, though their conversations had not got more fluent and the ardour between them had not kindled noticeably. They still basically had nothing to say to each other.

149

But Ruffo was not losing hope. He was as enthusiastic a gatherer of information as Isadora del Plato, and he chronicled everything in the dossier which would revolutionise the stuffy world of British journalism.

He was in the right place at the right time. With every day that passed, the prospects for the conflict starting became rosier. The government forces were massing on the borders of Jalapeno, and General Henriquez Guiteras seemed also to be drawing up his battle-lines. Every minute brought new rumours about which of his avowed supporters were likely to betray him. War was imminent. Ruffo felt thrillingly alive.

And, with the prospect of jeopardy, the attraction between him and Estrella grew. Soon there would come a night when their chances of survival the next day were negligible.

And that was when, Ruffo knew, their love would find its fullest expression.

Corky kept the headlights dowsed as he drove the Lagonda to where Isadora del Plato had directed them. It hadn't occurred to Blotto that, for someone whose apparent speciality was gathering information about international incidents, she had an exceptional knowledge of the underground cave systems of Jalapeno Province. All that concerned him was that she had given him an access route to Lazy Iguana Ranch.

Isadora had recommended that they equip themselves with electric torches and crowbars. Which they had done. With those, and his trusty cricket bat, Blotto reckoned he was ready for anything Colonel Pedro Jiminez could throw at him.

Corky Froggett was relieved that the cave entrance which had been pinpointed was out of rifle range of the compound. He didn't like the idea of leaving the precious Lag where its bodywork might suffer the attentions of a stray bullet – or indeed a targeted one.

Following Isadora del Plato's instructions, they didn't switch on the torches until they were safely underground. Given the pre-conflict tension, security around the compound would be at a high level.

The caves through which they walked became a kind of tunnel. They had formed naturally but, here and there, there was evidence of human activity, prominent rocks smashed out of the way, narrow passageways widened by the application of sledgehammers. The level of dust and proliferation of cobwebs suggested that no one had used the entrance for many decades. Again, Blotto didn't ask himself why Isadora del Plato might know of the cave system's existence when the residents of Lazy Iguana Ranch, living right on top of it, appeared not to.

'So, milord,' the chauffeur whispered, 'is the plan that we bring Lady Honoria out by the same route?'

'Bong on the nose, Corky. Along with her poor little greengage of a chumbo, Begonia.'

'Very good, milord. And do you have information as to where in the compound the two of them might be incarcerated?'

'According to my sources . . .' Blotto knew that Corky knew full well who his source was, but he quite enjoyed sounding mysterious every once in a while. 'According to my sources, the exit from the cave system is very near the old lockup which Colonel Pedro Jiminez has traditionally used as a clinkbox.'

'Excellent, milord,' said Corky. 'Pity we didn't bring some of Accrington-Murphy's best with us, in case some kind of dust-up develops.'

'Don't don your worry-boots about that,' said Blotto. 'I've got my cricket bat.'

Whoever had streamlined the tunnel had done a good job. Their progress was speedy and easy. Soon they found themselves facing an old, dusty set of steps which had been hewn some generations before out of the living rock.

All they had to do was find the exit.

It was dark and hot in the lockup where Twinks had been sent to join Begonia. Very little ventilation, and the air that did make its way in smelt heavily of animal excrement. There were two heavily locked double doors, the one through which she had been shoved in and another opposite.

Though the Mexican girl's spirits had been lifted by the arrival of her friend, they did not stay up for long. Begonia could see no happy outcome from her current situation. Her main ambition, to be reunited with Carlos Contreras, seemed further off than ever.

Twinks, eternally optimistic, made a great job of bolstering her friend's spirits. Everything, she assured Begonia, would soon be splendissimo. 'Blotto,' she said, 'will have tuned up the brainbox to find a way round this problemette. My bro always comes up with a beezer wheeze to get out of any treacle tin.'

But even as she said the words, looking around the thick stone walls of their prison, she could see no immediate solution, no means of extrication from this particular gluepot. And the idea of Blotto having any kind of wheeze, let alone a beezer one, to sort out any situation was, as his sister knew all too well, frankly laughable.

Though Twinks's lies seemed to have calmed Begonia, the prisoners' peace was also disturbed by strange noises. From the other side of the door opposite the entrance. Scuttling noises. A bit like claws scratching against stone. Or even against wire netting.

Begonia was at first frightened by the sounds, but Twinks reassured her that they were just branches in the wind, scraping against the walls of their prison. Fortunately, the younger woman believed her.

But Twinks knew she had been lying. She knew all too well what was making the noises the other side of the wall.

And the knowledge didn't make her think that everything was really splendissimo.

Blotto and Corky's torch beams illuminated what looked like a solid rockface in front of them. There was no telltale crack or uneven edge to indicate that it had ever contained an opening.

'It looks, milord,' said the chauffeur, 'as though we should have brought the pickaxes, rather than crowbars, to break the wall down.' That was, after all, how he had effected Blotto and Twinks's escape from General Guiteras's prison. 'Would you like me to go back to the Lag to fetch them, milord?'

'Rein in the roans for a moment, Corky. There's another solutionette that might be worth running up the mainmast.'

For once, for one rare moment, Blotto's logic was working impeccably. He had reasoned that the human handiwork in the caves under the Lazy Iguana Ranch was similar in style to that he had seen in the Attatotalloss Caves where Professor Hector Troon-Wheatley was excavating. Didn't that make it possible that the two were the work of the same group of people? And that they might be using the same techniques?

He ran his torch beam along the walls either side of the one which blocked their path. There were quite a few protuberances in the rock. He tried two to see if they would

153

shift or turn but they demonstrated rock's traditional quality of immovability.

The third one, though, gave under his hand. He twisted it a quarter turn to the right and, with the same sound as of grinding coffee, a rectangular opening appeared in the wall in front of them.

'Milord,' said the chauffeur, 'I keep thinking I have seen the full extent of your genius . . .' (Which, to be fair, in the view of many people, would not have been very extensive) '. . . and then you do something which makes me realise you are more brilliant than I thought.'

'Oh, really, Corky,' said a blushing Blotto. 'Don't talk such meringue.'

To save further embarrassment, Blotto immediately led the way out of the caves. The reason the entrance had been undiscovered for so long was apparent in the pale moonlight. It opened high into the wall of a blocked-up well. If there was a matching handle to open from the ranch side, its location had been long forgotten. Since Blotto and Corky could not see any sign of it, they shrewdly didn't attempt to close the entrance to the caves. They just climbed up to ground level.

As Isadora del Plato had promised, they found themselves very near the entrance to the lockup. There was no sign of any guards – or anyone else, come to that. And opening the prison doors did not even require the crowbars. They were locked simply by two metal bars, slid into double slots on each side. Impossible to shift from inside the lockup. But from outside, the bars slipped out as easily as they had slipped in.

Blotto and Corky's torch beams illuminated two shocked young women, standing defiantly side by side. Whatever fate awaited them, their bodies seemed to say, they were ready for it.

Corky had the bright idea of turning the torch towards

his face, so that the women could see they were rescuers, not murderers. Blotto followed suit, with a cry of, 'Twinkers! Beggers! We have arrived, just like the cavalry that didn't arrive for the Last Stand of General Custard!'

'Custer,' said Twinks instinctively.

'Good ticket.'

Then his sister cried triumphantly, 'Splendissimo! See, Begonia, I told you Blotters would have a beezer wheeze to get out of any treacle tin!'

Here was another occasion which, if it had been replayed a century later, would have involved much falling into each other's arms and hugging from the participants. But, since it was happening round 1930 amongst people of breeding, Blotto and Twinks just stood in silence, gazing at each other in mutual delight.

Unfortunately, this rapt admiration lasted a moment too long. Too late, all four of them turned at the sound of the open doors of the lockup being closed and the locking bars being slotted into place.

Hardly had this registered, before they heard bars being slotted out of the other doors and their being opened. The pale moonlight revealed a compound made of wire netting.

And, within seconds, their prison was filled with giant, man-eating, black iguanas.

Iguanas and Other Killers

They weren't to know the detail with which their come-uppance had been planned. Colonel Pedro Jiminez had been certain that Blotto would make an attempt to rescue his sister. Indeed, that was the sole reason why he had captured her. It was just a matter of waiting until the attempt was made.

Jiminez didn't know that Blotto and Corky would get into Lazy Iguana Ranch via the system of cave tunnels. Indeed, he didn't know that route existed. He had bought a certain amount of information from Isadora del Plato, but she hadn't vouchsafed him that particular nugget.

But he felt certain Blotto and Corky would break into the compound somehow. And, once inside, even if they hadn't been told where it was, they'd quickly find the lockup where the two prisoners were being held. The Colonel's soldiers, guards and peons had all been told to keep out of sight when the news came from one of his spies that the intruders were inside Lazy Iguana Ranch.

Even then, there was not to be a major assault. The Colonel's orders were that four guards should hide to watch the entrance to the lockup. Once Blotto and Corky had entered, two of them had been given orders to lock the front doors on them. And the other two were instructed to open the doors leading to the wire-netting-fenced compound beyond.

Then the guards' duties would be ended. The iguanas could be relied on to do the rest.

It was the kind of situation Blotto and Twinks relished. Immediate danger and impossible odds. He had of course seen the iguanas when he rescued her the time before from the clutches of Colonel Pedro Jiminez, so he knew what he was up against. And he reckoned he was armed with the perfect weapon. A cricket bat could have been designed to deal with man-eating iguanas. For an idle moment, as he fought them off, Blotto wondered if that *was* what it had been designed for. But decided, on the balance of probabilities, that it probably wasn't.

Corky Froggett had his electric torch and also picked up a plank of wood. With one in each hand, he felt equally well equipped to deal with the encroaching reptiles.

Even Begonia, devoted to animals as she was and a firm believer that none should ever be harmed, recognised that there were times when exceptions should be made to all principles. Picking up another plank, she proceeded to belabour the Iguanidae.

Twinks, however, did not join the defensive effort (though her sequined reticule, of course, contained plenty of suitable weaponry). Instead, using the reticule itself as a kind of swinging mace, she made her way through the advancing throng into their protective compound.

Once there, she reached into her sequined reticule and produced a pair of heavy-duty bolt cutters. She proceeded to cut out a door-shaped exit on the side nearest the cave entrance. Then, wielding the bolt cutters in one hand and the sequined reticule in the other, she windmilled her way back into the fray to lead her companions to safety.

She was pleased to see they were giving a good account of themselves. Obviously, the pile of iguanas in front of Blotto was the highest, all of them having been battered by his trusty willow from the Oval to Lord's via Edgbaston. But Corky Froggett's torch and plank had been doing some pretty good destruction work too. And Begonia, who had never in her life voluntarily injured an animal, was demonstrating a surprising aptitude for the task.

As she approached them, Twinks cried out, 'Come on! We must shift our shimmies and put a jumping cracker under it! Time to get our cloaks and follow the Way Out sign!'

'Oh, can't we linger a little longer?' asked an aggrieved Blotto. 'Fighting off these fumacious sponge-worms really is the lark's larynx.' He had been missing his hunting while he was out in Mexico.

'No!' said Twinks firmly, for a moment totally Dowager Duchess of Lyminster. 'Do as you're told, Blotto!'

Meekly acknowledging a superior power, Blotto obeyed instructions. Scattering black iguanas as he progressed, he made his way in the direction his sister indicated. Corky Froggett and Begonia Guiteras, also wreaking further havoc on their reptilian attackers, followed suit.

The four of them, still battling the stream of pursuing iguanas, made their way through the hole in the wire that Twinks had cut. And ran towards the cave entrance.

Only to find that, standing in their way, stood Colonel Pedro Jiminez, with serious-looking Accrington-Murphy revolvers in each hand.

'Not so fast,' he said. 'I have only to wound one of you in the arm or leg. The smell of blood will drive the iguanas mad. You will not be able to resist their power then!'

'What a load of plipping plankton!' said Twinks casually. 'The same would go for your blood too, Colonel.'

Lazily, she picked up a particularly large iguana and threw it straight at their captor's chest. His arms impeded by the guns he was carrying, Jiminez did not have time to take evasive action. Fearful of falling, the airborne iguana clutched at the front of his uniform, claws shredding the fabric and drawing blood from the flesh behind. Red dripped into the dust.

Instantly, the iguanas stopped in mid-action. Lifting their beaky snouts, they sniffed the air. And suddenly changed direction. Ignoring the foursome they had been attacking, they turned as one towards the Colonel.

The last thing Blotto and company saw, before they hurried back down into their cave escape route, was the iguanas' owner running to save his life. And his murderous charges avidly following the track of his bloodstains.

Life was definitely improving for Willy 'Ruffo' Walberswick. He had managed to infiltrate himself into the army of the Partido Nacional Revolucionario. As he had told El Chipito, he told everyone else that he was a journalist, but the majority suspected he was a spy. That allegation had only to be spoken out loud once and he would be dragged off to face an immediate firing squad.

Even if the assertion of his profession was believed, that didn't improve his prospects much. In this region, respect for journalists was low. The idea that accreditation from some foreign news desk gave them any kind of immunity was treated with derision. And the combatants weren't that keen on their activities being reported, anyway. If any account of the war was to be written, it should be done by the victors – or those who said they were the victors. Independent journalists were far too likely to chronicle defeats and atrocities. Many soldiers were of the view that just identifying oneself as a member of the Press was quite sufficient justification for a summary despatch by firing squad.

As he marched through the night with the Partido Nacional Revolucionario forces, it was difficult to imagine a scenario in which Willy 'Ruffo' Walberswick could have been in more danger. The idea thrilled him to bits. If only his red-haired vamp Estrella was with him.

Once the four escapees were out of the caves and safely in the Lagonda, there was a brief conversation as to where they should go next. Obviously, all Begonia Guiteras wanted to do was to be reunited with Carlos Contreras. But did anyone know precisely where he was?

'Last time I clapped my peepers on that particular slice of redcurrant cheesecake,' said Twinks, 'Blotters was about to hand him over to some thugbludgeon called El Chipito.'

'I have heard my father talk of him,' said Begonia. 'He is the leader of the government forces. Carlos will be with them now.'

'Good ticket,' said Blotto. 'Because apparently the balloon's tearing free of its spoffing guy-ropes any moment now.'

'Then why is this a good ticket?' asked Begonia.

'Because your Carlos boddo will be coming in this direction. You won't have to pongle halfway across the country to find him.'

'Yes, but he will be coming here to fight. Against my father. Both of the men who are closest to me will be in danger.'

Before this conversation about wartime jeopardy could proceed further, Twinks noticed something out of the window of the Lagonda. In the darkness, a darker shadow seemed to be flying alongside the great car.

'Stop, Corky!' she cried. 'There's something we need to check.'

Obedient as ever, the chauffeur brought their vehicle to a dusty halt. Twinks opened her back door and got out into the Mexican night. Knowing the right thing to do, she held out her slender silk-clad arm. Isadora del Plato's toucan perched on it.

Twinks reached for the small metal cylinder, which she removed from the bird's leg. She unscrewed it and quickly read the message on the thin paper inside.

'Spoffing useful information from Isadora del Plato,' she announced. 'Which, as I knew it would, answers our questionette about where we pongle off to next.'

'I didn't know you'd ever even clapped your peepers on Isadora del Plato,' said Blotto.

'I make it my business to truffle out the best sources of information, whatever country I'm in,' said Twinks crisply.

'So, where does the Spanish breath-sapper want us to turn our compass?' asked Blotto.

'Her message reads: "El Chipito's Partido Nacional Revolucionario forces have left Jalapeno City and are camped twenty miles from the Guiteras Ranch. For you, things are about to kick off at the Attatotalloss Caves. Be there at first light tomorrow."'

Taking the requisite pen and paper out of her sequined reticule, Twinks wrote a hasty note of reply and replaced it in the metal cylinder. With a whispered word to the toucan, she sent it on its way.

'Larksissimo!' she said, as she got back into the rear seat of the Lagonda. 'The fireworks of fun are about to be lit!'

Before she closed the car door, something dropped off the closed roof into the interior, landing on Begonia. The girl let out a little scream.

'What's the bizz-buzz?' asked Blotto from the front passenger seat.

'I'll check,' said Twinks, taking an electric torch out of her sequined reticule and turning it on Begonia's lap.

The beam revealed a small black iguana. Not much more than a baby, really.

'I'll deal with this, milord,' said Corky Froggett. 'It will give me great pleasure to coffinate the little monster.' And he opened the car door to go round and make good his word.

But he was stopped by a soft voice saying, 'No, don't hurt it.' After her recent, atypical violence, Begonia Guiteras's instinctive love for animals had returned. 'I'm going to keep it as a pet, an addition to my menagerie.'

No one in the car argued. Blotto took over the driving from Corky. They now had a deadline and a destination.

Dawn at the Attatotalloss Caves.

El Chipito's forces, and Willy 'Ruffo' Walberswick with them, were now inside Jalapeno Province, marching steadily towards the Guiteras Ranch, the stronghold of their rebel enemy. Their mercenary leader had told them to travel through the night, so as to surprise their enemy at dawn, when the hostilities would commence.

But then, suddenly, El Chipito countermanded the order. His men were told to pitch camp some twenty miles from their adversary. No reason was given for the change of strategy.

The reason was only known to El Chipito himself. He had received a message, courtesy of Isadora del Plato's toucan, which altered his priorities. It told him he would never have a better opportunity than that dawn at the Attatotalloss Caves. To kill Blotto.

* * *

At the Guiteras Ranch, the General was also checking his preparations for the forthcoming conflict. His spies – including Isadora del Plato – had kept him well up to speed with what was happening in the enemy camp. He knew of El Chipito's plans to surprise him at dawn. And he was excited by the prospect of imminent bloodshed.

A few things niggled at him, though. He wasn't sure how much he could trust Pedro Jiminez. The Colonel had assured him of his undying loyalty with so much vehemence that it made him suspicious. Guiteras was equally unsure of the fealty of the other wealthy land-owners of Jalapeno Province. They too had given stout assurances of support. But if any of them wavered and allied their better-trained soldiers to El Chipito's ragbag army, the outcome could prove distinctly uncomfortable.

The other thing that still rankled with General Henriquez Guiteras was the escape from his custody of Blotto and Twinks. He didn't like to be made to look a fool and he passionately wanted revenge.

So, it was timely when he received a message, courtesy of Isadora del Plato's toucan, announcing El Chipito's postponement of his attack. And the reason for it.

She also told him he would never have a better opportunity than that dawn at the Attatotalloss Caves. To kill Blotto.

El Falleza didn't need the intervention of the toucan. He had the information direct from the mouth of his inamorata.

Isadora told him he would never have a better opportunity than that dawn at the Attatotalloss Caves. To kill Blotto.

* * *

Colonel Pedro Jiminez had never expected to be the quarry of his specially trained black iguanas. He hadn't considered the possibility that it might be his own blood which drove them to homicidal frenzy. It was only by shouting for help from his heavily weaponed private army that he had managed to survive their onslaught. He was left considerably shaken, his body much scarred with claw marks and beak bites.

He was also left with an unassuageable thirst for revenge.

So, he was ecstatic to receive a message from Isadora del Plato's toucan, telling him he would never have a better opportunity than that dawn at the Attatotalloss Caves. To kill Blotto.

The other person who had expressed a wish to kill our fine upstanding hero, the gun-runner Sydney Pollard, had changed his priorities. All he wanted to do was to get as far away from Jalapeno Province as possible. He had plans to get the first possible liner from Veracruz to take him to the next 'international incident'. Where he would once again arrange the purchase of his splendid Accrington-Murphy wares by representatives of both sides.

Inside his tent in the Partido Nacional Revolucionario encampment, Willy 'Ruffo' Walberswick made a pretence at preparing for bed. He had little prospect of sleeping. His jeopardy was too excitingly intense.

He was alerted by the scrape of a fingernail on the canvas and a soft voice murmuring, 'Ruffo?'

He picked up his Accrington-Murphy revolver and cautiously drew aside the tent flap, fully prepared for a fusillade of bullets.

What greeted him instead was much more sensational. Estrella. Flame-haired Estrella.

She smiled at him coyly. 'Ruffo, El Chipito has gone out and left me alone in our tent. If he were to find out that another man had joined me in the bed there, I dare not imagine the kind of revenge El Chipito would take on him.'

Willy 'Ruffo' Walberswick had never been so aroused in his life, as he followed Estrella through the encampment to the relevant tent.

17

Dawn at the Attatotalloss Caves

Professor Hector Troon-Wheatley was very excited as he arrived that day, before dawn, at the Attatotalloss Caves. Though he had enjoyed Twinks's company and assistance, for his excavations to progress at speed he needed more manpower. There was a lot of heavy lifting and digging to be done before he could reveal the evidence which would prove his theories and set the tectonic plates of the archaeological establishment shuddering.

And Troon-Wheatley had heard from the gangmaster Refritos that his team had been persuaded they no longer had anything to fear from the Curse of Attatotalloss. They would all be returning to work that morning.

He saw no reason any longer to keep secret his discovery of the lower level of the caves. That was where he wanted Refritos's peons to be working, so they'd find out about it soon enough, anyway. With practised ease, he twisted the relevant protrusion of rock and watched the antique but durable engineering do its stuff. The staircase appeared. Troon-Wheatley descended the steps and lit candles in the space below. Then he sat down and waited for his workforce to arrive.

The Professor looked forward to a constructive and rewarding day.

The Lagonda was still some miles away from the caves when Refritos arrived there with his gang of peons. Professor Hector Troon-Wheatley was surprised that none of them showed any reaction to the stairs which had been revealed leading down to the lower level. But then, of course, he didn't know that they had spent time during his absences stowing crates labelled as 'Pollard's Corned Beef' down there.

Anyway, he set them to work first on the top level of the caves. A lot of sand had blown in in the last few days and it needed clearing. While his men got on with the work, the gangmaster Refritos lay under his mule-cart, smoking a cigarillo. Beside him, close enough for him to keep an eye on it, was a stout leather bag, containing a bulky roundish object.

There was a good hour to go before dawn when the Lagonda turned on to the dusty track which wound some half-dozen tortuous miles up to the Attatotalloss Caves. Twinks, who both men in the car took for granted would be giving the instructions, told them what would happen next.

'The most important thing on our to-dos is to get those two lovebuds, Begonia and Carlos, back under the same umbrella. So, you, Corky, are to drive the Lag back towards Jalapeno City till you find El Chipito's encampment. Hand Begonia over to Carlos, neat as a Royal Mail parcel, then come back here to the caves.'

'Very good, milady,' he said. Then had the nerve to put

167

a question. 'Are you sure you and the young master will be safe going into the caves alone?'

'Do the French like cheese?' asked Twinks derisively. 'We'll be as safe as two bugs in a bugbed.'

'But, milady, don't you think you should take a couple of Accrington-Murphy revolvers?'

'Corky, me old tin of pickled halibut,' said Blotto, 'I will have my cricket bat with me.'

'And I,' said Twinks, 'have a variety of useful armaments in my sequined reticule.'

The chauffeur knew there was no point in arguing further.

It wasn't yet dawn, but the darkness of the night had diluted a little. Refritos watched the approach of the Lagonda. He hadn't met Blotto or Twinks, but he'd heard about the arrival of the English intruders and had no difficulty identifying them. Two blond siblings, one magnificently muscular, the other seductively sylphlike, were rare sights in Jalapeno Province.

When they all got out of the car, Begonia decided she'd sit in the front next to Corky Froggett on the journey to meet her lover. The baby black iguana, with whom she had bonded on the journey and christened Luna, was keen to go with her.

'I don't think I'd better take Luna,' said Begonia. 'I'm not sure that a battlefield is a good place for a pet.'

'Probably not,' Twinks agreed.

'Could you look after her for me?'

Every instinct said this was a bad idea, but the appeal in Begonia's brown eyes was so soulful that Twinks said, 'Tickey-tockey', and put the creature into her sequined reticule.

Then, with a stiff smile from Corky Froggett and an excited wave from Begonia Guiteras, the Lagonda set off on its romantic mission.

Though the blond siblings might have constituted an unusual sight in Mexico, the peons labouring at the ground level of the caves showed no interest at all in them. They just got on with doing what they were told.

Blotto and Twinks descended the stairs to be greeted by Professor Hector Troon-Wheatley. He looked as handsome and anxious as ever, and clearly didn't welcome Blotto's presence. Twinks he regarded as a bona fide archaeological professional. Her brother, so far as he knew, had no advanced academic credentials.

But the Professor could recognise there was no point in trying to get rid of the young man. The morning's task was not one that required any specialised knowledge. The rubble that had hidden the crates of corned beef/Accrington-Murphy armaments had all now been catalogued and cleared, so the space was completely empty.

'I'm convinced,' said Troon-Wheatley, 'that somewhere in here is an entrance to another cave system. And, working on the assumption that whoever hid it used the same principles as they did for the entrance down into this area, I think there could well be another unlocking device disguised as a protuberant piece of rock. All we've got to do is find it.'

The three of them looked round the cave, lit by flickering candles. Every surface was pockmarked with protuberant pieces of rock. It was going to be a long day.

The Professor divided the area into three and enjoined his helpers to start trying to turn every bit of rock that stuck out. Twinks felt confident that this was an instruction even Blotto wouldn't have difficulty in following.

But before they started, she had a question. 'Heckie, me old bit of pocket fluff, is anything else on the bill of fare for this morning?'

'What do you mean?'

'Well, I received a message telling me that something was going to "kick off" in the Attatotalloss Caves at dawn this morning. Do you know what it was referring to?'

'Absolutely no idea,' said Professor Hector Troon-Wheatley.

Corky Froggett thought he was going to be in for a rough ride when he arrived at the outskirts of the Partido Nacional Revolucionario encampment. The guards were suspicious of any arrivals, particularly ones who came in a blue Lagonda and didn't speak any Spanish. Both sides had elaborate spy networks and Corky fitted the profile of a secret agent all too well.

It was only when Begonia Guiteras identified herself that the hostile atmosphere eased. The fact that the daughter of their adversaries' commanding officer was handing herself over voluntarily seemed a promising development. Maybe she was prepared to betray her father's battle plans. Begonia, with Corky Froggett in tow, was taken at once to the tent where the Partido Nacional Revolucionario top brass were devising their strategy.

For reasons that Corky Froggett could not know, El Chipito was not among their number. (Indeed, if he had known the reasons, he would have hightailed straight back to the Attatotalloss Caves to defend the young master.)

But General Ignacio Contreras, the ousted governor of Jalapeno Province, was present. And, more important from the point of view of Begonia Guiteras, so was his son Carlos.

The scene as the two young lovers fell into each other's arms was very touching. Corky Froggett had never, in his entire life, shed a manly tear but, if he ever did have cause to, this might have been one of those moments.

As he drove back in the Lagonda, he felt warmed by the part he had played in reuniting Begonia and Carlos. And he reflected on the contrast between their innocent adoration and his more complicated love-life. That brought to mind the image of Carmelita. And he felt enormous relief at the thought that he would never have to see her again.

Little knowing that Carmelita herself had other plans. No one slighted her and got away with it.

Begonia and Carlos's romance was not the only one to be featured in the Partido Nacional Revolucionario encampment. At the same time, Willy 'Ruffo' Walberswick and Estrella were enjoying the greatest night of passion either of them had ever experienced.

As they parted outside El Chipito's tent, Estrella said, 'I will remember this for all my life. Which won't actually be very long, once El Chipito finds out what's happened.'

'You can say that again,' commented an unexpected voice.

They saw, lit by the flames of a campfire, a soldier sitting on the ground cleaning his rifle.

'If you think,' he went on, 'anyone here's going to keep quiet about what we've all witnessed, then you're very definitely barking up the wrong tree. El Chipito will be informed the minute he gets back.'

Ruffo responded by kissing Estrella full on the lips. It was a gesture of farewell, but also another piece of evidence, for anyone who happened to be watching, of their betrayal of El Chipito.

He returned to his own tent in a state of high excitement. Double jeopardy. Danger from El Chipito's return. And, if he survived that, alternative danger from the prospect of being killed in the bloody battle ahead.

Willy 'Ruffo' Walberswick felt ecstatic.

From his vantage point beneath the mule-cart, Refritos could see all of the arrivals at the Attatotalloss Caves. And there were a good few of them. All on horseback.

First came General Henriquez Guiteras, magnificent in his uniform, the dawn light glinting off its gilded epaulettes and tassels. Refritos reflected that, had the General arrived a mere half an hour earlier, he might have been reunited with his missing daughter.

Guiteras dismounted and tied his horse to a tree. He was about to enter the cave complex when he heard the sound of approaching hoofs. Looking across the plain, he saw the unmistakable figure of El Chipito galloping towards him.

He waited until the mercenary had also moored his horse, then addressed him. 'Shouldn't we be meeting on a battlefield, rather than here?'

El Chipito smiled, breaking the line of his scar. 'We will, Guiteras, we will. But I have a more important duty to discharge first.'

'Me too. Which is why I am here at the Attatotalloss Caves.'

El Chipito looked surprised. 'I was told that it was here that I would find my quarry.'

'I received the same information.'

'Is it possible,' asked the mercenary, 'that we are both seeking to kill the same man?'

They soon discovered that it was. And so began an argument about which of them should have the honour of despatching Blotto, with claims and counterclaims on the lines of 'I saw him first!'

How long this playground toing and froing might have continued it is impossible to say because it was interrupted by the arrival on horseback of El Falleza. When it became clear that the bullfighter was on the same mission as the others, keen to finish off Blotto with his matador's sword, the two-sided argument developed into a three-hander.

'We will have the advantage over you, El Falleza,' said General Henriquez Guiteras at one point. 'By the time you get close enough to the bounder to stab, we will have shot him.'

'I don't deny,' said the bullfighter, 'that I would much rather despatch him like a *toro*, but I am prepared to compromise to obtain the satisfaction of being his killer.' And he drew a revolver from inside his jacket.

'Well then,' said the General, brandishing his own revolver, 'it's a matter of who gets to the victim first!'

The three of them started to run into the caves but were interrupted by the arrival, at high speed, of a red Hispano-Suiza. Out of the dust cloud caused by its sudden braking stepped a scarred and angry Colonel Pedro Jiminez.

'What are you lot doing here?' he demanded. 'I have come to kill the notorious Englishman who goes under the ridiculous name of Blotto!'

Needless to say, this announcement escalated into a four-way argument between the aspirant murderers.

It was General Henriquez Guiteras who came up with the solution. 'Stop! Stop!' he cried. 'We will never agree on this. The killing of this blot on the landscape is too important to each of us to let any of the others claim to have done the deed. When I held him in captivity at the Guiteras Ranch, my plan was to have him executed by firing squad. That must be the way we do it. Inside the caves, the four of us will all line up and fire at the same time. Then we will not know which one of us fired the fatal bullet, but each of us can take credit for it.'

None of the others was entirely happy with this suggestion. Every one of them really wanted to claim Blotto's scalp as their own. But they recognised that Guiteras had put forward the only workable way round the problem.

Checking their revolvers, the four men entered the Attatotalloss Caves on their murderous mission.

Thinking the situation looked interesting, Refritos picked himself up from under the mule-cart and, gathering his leather bag, followed them in.

18

The Secrets of Attatotalloss

As he brought the Lagonda to a halt outside the cave entrance, Corky Froggett was surprised to see the tethered horses and the red Hispano-Suiza.

He was even more surprised to see a small female figure come bursting out of the undergrowth, carrying a massive cooking pot. Shouting furious imprecations, she put the pot down and, using a large ladle, started hurling its contents at the bemused chauffeur.

Corky Froggett recognised Carmelita immediately, though of course he had no idea what she was shouting. And, as a large hot splat of the stuff hit his face, he also recognised the unmistakable smell of refried beans.

The makeshift firing squad of four stood at one end of the lower cave. Behind them lurked an intrigued Refritos. At the other end stood a defiant Blotto, his cricket bat at the ready, as though it would have no problem batting away the approaching bullets. Twinks stood sturdily beside him, on her face the expression of redoubtable stoicism which the Lyminsters had worn at royal funerals from that of William the Conqueror onwards. Professor

Hector Troon-Wheatley havered in the middle of the cave, between the imminent fusillade and its targets.

'I would advise you to get out of the way,' General Henriquez Guiteras said to him. '*We* will not be concerned if we kill you too, but you might be.'

After an anguished look at Twinks, the Professor turned his back on her and scuttled behind the line of fire to where Refritos was standing with his bag. Troon-Wheatley didn't want to die before his discoveries had definitively disproved the theories of many rival archaeologists. And before he had seen the looks of fury on their faces. Getting one up on their rivals was, after all, the sole aim of all academics.

Colonel Pedro Jiminez also addressed Twinks. 'You don't have to die with your brother,' he said. 'Come to this side of the cave. We have no argument with you.' Maybe he was nursing the hope that a subdued and bereaved Twinks might prove more biddable and agree to the idea of marrying him.

But if he thought that, he'd chosen the wrong woman. 'If you imagine,' said Twinks magnificently, 'that a Lyminster would sell a family member up the river for a handful of winkle shells, then you know nothing of our glorious history. Lyminsters have proved themselves to be Grade A foundation stones for other Lyminsters through the centuries, in the Crusades, during the Wars of the Roses, the Civil War, the Restoration, any number of foreign wars, gymkhanas and ping-pong matches—'

She could have continued in this vein for hours and hours, but General Henriquez Guiteras suspected that she was just playing for time (which of course she was) and interrupted her flow with a cry of: 'Enough of this! We don't have time to waste. El Chipito and I are about to go to war with each other. Come on, firing squad, raise your weapons!'

'Just a moment,' said Twinks in a commanding tone. 'In every civilised country, a person who has been found guilty and sentenced to die by firing squad is always granted a last request.'

'We do not have time for this!' roared the General.

'I think we do,' argued Pedro Jiminez. Possibly still hoping to end up with Twinks.

'Very well,' Guiteras conceded grumpily. 'What is your last request?'

'Oh, I don't really think we need one,' said Blotto, with a debonair grin. 'It'll all be creamy éclair. I've got my cricket bat.'

Ignoring her brother, Twinks replied to the General, 'I don't want to break beyond the boundaries on this. Toeing the traditional line, Blotto and I would both like to smoke a final cigarette.'

'But neither of us—' Blotto objected. Then, seeing the expression on his sibling's face, he didn't continue saying they were both non-smokers. Instead, he mumbled out, 'Neither of us would think it was the panda's panties to face a fumacious firing squad without having guffed a last gasper.'

'I think we should let them do it, General,' said Jiminez, still hopeful about his chances with Twinks.

'All right,' said Guiteras peevishly. 'But smoke the bloody things quickly!'

'I've got the whole ciggie rombooley, the lighters and the lighted, in here,' said Twinks, reaching inside her sequined reticule.

The chief shame engendered by Carmelita's refried beans onslaught was what it was doing to Corky Froggett's uniform. An offence to his livery was an affront to the fine old family of Lyminster. Escaping the battery by going away from the caves was, for Corky, out of the question. It raised the serious risk of some of the noxious purée landing on the sacred bodywork of the young master's Lagonda, perhaps an even greater affront to the fine old family of Lyminster. His only possible route of avoidance was going into the caves.

Dawn, by then, had definitely broken. The rising sun silhouetted the chauffeur in the entrance.

Now, everyone grows up with some beliefs, some stories which they've been told as children and which they've never quite got out of the habit of believing. If you had grown up in a peon family in the Jalapeno Province of Mexico in the early part of the twentieth century, among those beliefs or stories would be the following:

'In Aztec times there was a great God King called Attatotalloss, who was mightily powerful and fabulously wealthy. When he died, he was buried with enormous pomp and riches in an unknown venue. His tomb has never been found, though there are caves, here in Jalapeno Province, that are named after him. Superstition says that the reason his tomb has never been found is because it is guarded by the Ghost of Attatotalloss. Though no one who has seen the ghost has survived long to tell the tale, rumours abound that the figure has a black body, smeared with some kind of primeval mud, and wears a headdress with a kind of beak-like protuberance at the front. Anyone who does see the Ghost of Attatotalloss will, within a week, die in agony.'

Now, if you were a humble Mexican peon in Jalapeno Province who had grown up being fed that myth, and if you were to look up one morning from your work of clearing rubble from a cave and see, framed in the entrance, a black figure, smeared with a glutinous beige substance and wearing headgear with a peak in the front . . . your first thought might not be that you were looking at

Corky Froggett, a chauffeur from Tawcester Towers in the county of Tawcestershire in England.

And, indeed, that was not what the first peon to look towards the entrance of the Attatotalloss Caves that morning did think. When he saw a black figure, smeared with a glutinous beige substance and wearing headgear with a peak in the front, his first thought was that he had come face to face with the Ghost of Attatotalloss and would die in agony within the week.

And his first reaction was to let out a terrible scream. This caused his fellow workers to look to see what had caused the scream and, very soon, to join in. Their second reaction was to rush out, past the death-bearing ghost, into the open air, and to run. And not to stop running until they reached their homes. Where they would spend a very terrified seven days, waiting to die in agony.

Corky Froggett, a little confused by the peons' behaviour, walked on into the caves.

The cigarettes were almost burnt down to their lips. Twinks regretted that, if she really was about to die, she would die with such a revolting taste in her mouth. Blotto didn't contemplate dying. His cricket bat would see him all right.

So they stood, defiantly facing the firing squad, in a rather one-sided Mexican standoff.

'Right,' said General Henriquez Guiteras. 'Throw down the stubs!' Blotto and Twinks both did as instructed. 'Firing squad, raise your revolvers! Now, on a count of three . . .'

'Could we make it a count of ten?' asked Twinks, at her most charming.

'Why?'

'Just need to pop some gubbins in my sequined reticule.'

'Count of three it is,' insisted the General. 'One ... Two ...'

As Twinks opened her sequined reticule to put her lighter back in there, Luna, Begonia Guiteras's new pet, decided she'd had enough of being shut in. She leapt out of the sequined reticule and, clueless as to where she was, scuttled off across the cave's floor. Unsighted, she jumped upwards.

And landed on the chest of Refritos.

The gangmaster, taken totally off his guard, dropped his leather bag. The grenade inside it, on impact with the floor, exploded.

19

Untold Riches!

When the crashing of the rockfall subsided and the blinding dust began to settle, the first thing Blotto and Twinks realised was that they were both alive. It was another of those moments when any two people who hadn't been brought up the way they had would have fallen into each other's arms.

The next thing they became aware of was that the cave floor on which they stood was half the size it had been before. A large section opposite them had dropped away into the void beneath. Of General Henriquez Guiteras, El Chipito, Colonel Pedro Jiminez, El Falleza, Refritos and Professor Hector Troon-Wheatley, there was no sign.

Reassuringly, though, Luna, the baby iguana had managed, at the moment of explosion, to leap back towards them, on to the surviving half of the floor. Hiding its claws, it had climbed up Twinks, causing her no pain, and wrapped itself, in a confidential manner, around her slender neck.

'Larksissimo!' said Twinks.

'Toad-in-the-hole!' said Blotto.

Funny how the right words always came for the right occasion.

Professor Hector Troon-Wheatley shared with Blotto and Twinks the strange realisation that he was still alive. The shock of the explosion left him feeling as if the ground had disappeared beneath his feet. Which, of course, it had.

And he was tumbling and turning into nothingness. But then, suddenly, his hand brushed against something. He grabbed hold. It felt like a tree root. And it had the effect of halting his descent, though his bodyweight nearly pulled his arms out of their sockets.

Troon-Wheatley waited for a moment, until the screams and clatterings of the other free-fallers ceased, and then assessed his own situation. The darkness was not quite as total as he had first thought. There was a little glimmer of something from the opening high above his head. It provided enough light for him to confirm that what he was holding was a tree root. And also, that there were other tree roots protruding higher up the rockface. Laboriously, the Professor started to pull himself up.

Blotto and Twinks examined their altered surroundings. Remarkably, from the space excavated by Refritos's grenade, light emanated. Surely it must be natural light? Or had other humans been in the lower depths recently?

Gingerly, the siblings moved to the edge of the shattered floor and looked down. Yes, the light did appear to be natural, streaming from some unseen aperture in the rock. Wherever the opening was, it didn't face the same way as the main entrance to the Attatotalloss Caves.

The collapse of the floor had also exposed a staircase carved into the rock, which led downwards. There were no signs of any Victorian engineered portal to this. Twinks reckoned it was probably at least five hundred years since a human foot had touched those steps.

She and Blotto, the latter with cricket bat still firmly in hand, stepped easily on to them and started their descent into the mysterious space beneath.

Professor Hector Troon-Wheatley was finding it hard going. Rarely could he get any purchase on anything with his feet. His sore arms had to support his whole body-weight. Fortunately, a lifetime working in excavations had made him pretty fit.

As he looked upwards, he tried to work out what lay above. Light seemed to be coming, not from one source in the rockface, but two. Was it possible that the higher one was the level where the grenade had detonated? And the lower one the secret level of caves, of whose existence he had always been convinced? Had the explosion actually opened up the place where he would find the evidence to prove his theories? And wipe the smug smiles off the faces of all those rival academics who disagreed with him?

Buoyed up by this hope, the Professor's limbs found new energy to cope with the draining climb ahead.

Blotto and Twinks stood at the foot of the steps into the lowest cave in a state of stunned amazement.

The light source proved to be a round opening at the far end from the staircase. Through it could be seen palm trees and, further away, the outline of what might have been an ancient temple. Twinks's brain calculated that the opening must be very high up the mountain face on the far side from the Guiteras Ranch and probably invisible from the ground. Otherwise, the contents would not have remained undisturbed for so many centuries. The tomb-robbers would have found it.

The outside air formed a pleasant current which Twinks reckoned was the reason why the interior of the cave had not silted up with sand. The breeze had kept the dust moving.

If this cave was indeed, as it was rumoured to be, the tomb of the God King Attatotalloss, there was no evidence of a visible coffin or sarcophagus. There were unlimited numbers of tarnished metal statues scattered on the floor which, Twinks's wide knowledge of the period told her, had been used in Aztec religious ceremonies. The place would have been a treasure house for Professor Hector Troon-Wheatley.

The most striking object, though, mounted on a small shelf of rock, was a human skull, covered with dull stones. A flick of Twinks's silk scarf revealed the stones to be far from dull. With the dust removed, they shone and refracted the light in a way that only diamonds can.

'Great whiffling water rats!' said Twinks.

Her brother, equally impressed, said, 'Great galumphing goatherds! Would that be something elastic?'

'Aztec,' said Twinks automatically.

'Good ticket.'

'But it'd be quite a jaw-dropper if it was Aztec. They didn't go in for gubbins like that. I think there's been some backdoor fakery at work. Mind you,' Twinks went on, looking again at the skull, 'if those stones aren't leadpenny, that bonehead is worth an Arthur's ransom.'

But Blotto's eyes were already wandering towards another object on the cave floor. A dust-covered chest, its wood not yet rotted and its iron bounds showing little sign of rust.

'That looks like the real ginger,' said Blotto, moving towards it, now holding his cricket bat in his left hand.

'Bound to be full of the old jingle-jangle, don't you reckon, Twinks?' He reached his hand to the clasp.

'Rein in the roans, Blotters! The Conquistadors didn't sign in grave-robbing intruders on their guestlists. There's quite a possibilitette that they may have set up some security system to guard that chest.'

'What, you mean this poor greengage of a ghost? The black one dolloped with mud and wearing a pointy headdress?'

'No, I meant something more on the lines of a booby trap.'

'Oh, puddledash, Twinks! You're talking through your elbow patch!' said Blotto, as he reached again to touch the clasp of the chest.

It was as well that the speed of his reactions had been finely tuned on the cricket pitch. As he touched the chest, there was a twanging sound, similar to that the French might have heard at Crécy when the English bowmen unleashed their first volley. And a hail of small darts travelled at speed towards the target of Blotto. It was only his extreme dexterity with the cricket bat which enabled him to deflect them all.

A couple flew off the bat towards Twinks. One embedded itself in her pith helmet. The other Luna the baby iguana neatly caught in her teeth. Twinks removed it from her beak and sniffed the pointed end.

'Curare,' she pronounced.

'Why? What's wrong with him?' asked Blotto.

'What's wrong with who?'

'Aari. You just said, "Cure Aari".'

'No, I meant . . .' Twinks shook her head. 'Never mind, Blotters.'

'Well, let's see how much golden gravy there is in here!'

Blotto returned to the chest. Maybe whoever had set the

booby trap hadn't anticipated anyone surviving the hail of poisoned darts. There was certainly no lock to be seen.

But the raising of the lid did trigger one more surprise for those of a nervous disposition. Out of the opened chest there sallied a brigade of giant spiders. Blotto, who had never been of a nervous disposition, was unworried by them.

'What in the name of snitchrags are those, Twinks?' he asked, certain that his sister would be able to supply the answer.

His confidence was not misplaced, as Twinks replied, 'They are Arachnidae of the family Theraphosidae, known as *Theraphosa blondi* or, more commonly, Goliath Birdeaters.'

'Tickey-tockey,' said Blotto, who now had eyes only for what the removing of the blanket of spiders revealed. The chest was full to the brim with gold.

Not Aztec gold. There was nothing to be seen like the votive offerings Twinks had found in the other parts of the cave. This hoard was gold coins and gold jewellery. The metal from which they had been made might have been of pre-Columbian origin, but those artefacts had been melted down and reshaped into money and trinkets.

Blotto and Twinks had found the Conquistadors' gold!

Corky Froggett had spent some time in the empty ground-level cave, checking that Carmelita was not about to continue her onslaught inside. Once he felt secure about that, he tried to scrape some of the refried beans off his precious uniform. It was a thankless task. The goo seemed to have embedded itself into the black fabric.

Then, intrigued by the light glowing from below at the far end of the cave, he set out to investigate.

* * *

186

The Giant Birdeaters were still quite interested in Blotto and he had to keep batting them off as he examined the hoard of gold.

'There's enough here, O sister of mine,' he said, 'to sort out the Tawcester Towers plumbing for all eternity and considerably longer.'

'There is, O brother of mine,' Twinks agreed, 'except of course it doesn't belong to us.'

'You're bong on the nose there,' Blotto agreed ruefully. 'So, who does the whole clangdumble belong to?'

'According to the Mexican legal system,' replied Twinks, who knew about such things, 'which is currently in a total state of chaos because of the recent civil war, treasure trove is covered by a very old law which has never been repealed. And the person who finds the stuff has no rights in it at all. All treasure belongs to the person on whose land it is found. In this case, General Henriquez Guiteras.'

'Well, we don't want that four-faced filcher to get it, do we?'

'It's possible,' said Twinks gently, 'that that four-faced filcher is in no position to get it.'

For a moment, Blotto looked even blanker than usual. Then, slowly, enlightenment dawned. 'Oh, you mean the slugbucket might have been coffinated? That all of those lumps of toadspawn who wanted to coffinate us might have been coffinated themselves when the spoffing floor collapsed under them.'

'It's within the realms of reality,' said Twinks soberly.

Both were silent for a moment. Though the people who had fallen into the void had been on the point of acting as a firing squad and killing them, Blotto and Twinks didn't like to hear about the death of any individual. Whatever the situation, it could rather take the icing off the Swiss bun.

A sudden realisation brought Twinks's hand to her

mouth in a gasp of horror. 'And Heckie! Heckie was with them! If they've all been coffinated, then Heckie has too!'

'Tough Gorgonzola,' Blotto commiserated.

But, before further lamentations about his death could ensue, Professor Hector Troon-Wheatley got a grasp on the topmost tree root of his ascent and his head appeared over the edge of the void.

'Heckie!' cried an ecstatic Twinks. 'Splendissimo!'

Blotto ran forward to help the battered archaeologist up on to the cave floor.

He got no thanks. Troon-Wheatley was too stunned by the place where he found himself. 'I knew I was right!' he said. 'I knew this cave existed! The third level! Now I can prove all my theories about the Aztecs. I can wipe the patronising smiles off the faces of all those academics who believe they were hunter/gatherers who migrated from the north.'

Only then did he seem to take in the fact that Blotto and Twinks were also in the cave. 'Glad you're all right,' he said in a rather perfunctory manner. 'Last time I saw you, you were about to be killed by firing squad.'

'Oh, things like that,' said Blotto airily, 'for us are just like water off a duck's front.'

But Troon-Wheatley wasn't listening. He was on the floor, looking with delight at the sculpted artefacts there. 'This is wonderful,' he enthused. 'This will turn conventional thinking in archaeology completely on its head.'

He looked round suspiciously at Blotto and Twinks. 'You haven't touched anything, have you? Or moved anything? I need to record every object in the exact position where it was found.'

'We did dab the digits on something,' Twinks admitted.

'Oh, no!' cried the distraught Professor, burying his bearded face in his hands. 'What was it? What have you ruined?'

'Well, to be fair,' said Blotto, 'they were ruins already, so we didn't—'

Twinks cut him short. 'Only this tonky chest.'

The Professor dismissed it with a contemptuous glance. 'I'm not interested in that. Nothing pre-Columbian there. Well, the original gold may have been, but the Conquistadors melted it down and made it worthless for academic research.'

'And then,' said Blotto, 'there's something else that's a bit of a wonky donkey.' He pointed. 'A human skull covered with diamonds. Would that have been made by the Aspics?'

'Aztecs,' said Twinks automatically.

Troon-Wheatley's glance at the skull was even more dismissive than the one he'd cast on the chest. 'Good heavens, no! The Aztecs were people of sophisticated creativity. They had respect for art. What kind of taste-free Philistine would think a skull studded with diamonds had any artistic value?'

'So, what will you do with these things, Heckie?' asked Twinks. 'The chest and the skull?'

'Get rid of them as soon as possible. They'll just be in the way of my research.'

'When you say, "Get rid of them",' asked Twinks, 'do you mean send them to England for you to deal with when you get back there?'

'No!' Troon-Wheatley replied. 'Get rid of them! As I say, they're of no interest to me. I just want them out of here as soon as possible.'

'So,' Blotto suggested cautiously, 'if we were to take the chest and the skull out of the cave, we wouldn't be taking any cream off your strawberries?'

'Absolutely not! In fact, I'd be eternally grateful. The sooner you can get the wretched things out of here, the better, so far as I'm concerned.'

189

'And you don't care what happens to them?' asked Twinks, just to be sure.

'So far as I'm concerned,' said the Professor, 'you can drop them in the middle of the Atlantic Ocean!'

Blotto and Twinks exchanged looks. Yes, they had both heard him right. The goodies were theirs. Just the small matter of lifting the chest. 'We might need the muscle of that Grade A foundation stone, Corky Froggett,' said Blotto.

As if summoned by the mention of his name, the chauffeur appeared at that moment on the stairs from the upper level.

'Great toppling toadstools!' cried Twinks. 'What on earth's happened to your uniform, Corkers?'

But before he could make any reply, that uniform was suddenly covered with spiders. And Twinks remembered the little-known fact (she was very good at little-known facts missed by other experts) that Goliath Birdeaters have a particular taste for refried beans (as well as, obviously, for birds).

Within seconds, the spiders had sated themselves – like locusts stripping off every last vestige of Carmelita's assault weapons – and crawled away to sleep off their unexpected feast. Corky Froggett's uniform looked as if it had just returned from the dry cleaner's.

'Corky old man,' said Blotto, 'could you give me a bit of a heave-ho with this chest?'

As the two men carried their valuable load up to the next level, Twinks heard the fluttering of something entering the cave. Knowing immediately what to do, she stretched out her right arm, on to which Isadora del Plato's toucan gracefully landed.

She opened the metal cylinder. That morning's message read: 'Open warfare between the forces of El Chipito and

General Henriquez Guiteras will start today. For your own safety, it would be a good time for you to leave Mexico.'

Twinks was inclined to agree with this advice . . . just as soon as the chest of gold and the skull had been stowed in the secret compartment of the Lagonda.

Mind you, she could have corrected the message in the matter of El Chipito and General Henriquez Guiteras being in any state to start 'open warfare'.

Twinks got a considerable buzz from the fact that her own information service had proved more up to date than Isadora del Plato's.

20

War!

In an event so rare that it should be recorded in the annals of history, Twinks was wrong. The reputation of Isadora del Plato's information service remained intact.

It might have been thought that the four men making up the improvised firing squad in the Attatotalloss Caves would have been killed by Refritos's grenade. But, in fact, the stout leather bag in which he was keeping it did limit the spread of shrapnel to some extent. The impact of the explosion was sufficient to shatter the thin stone floor of the cave, but none of the revolver-bearers sustained more than superficial injuries. The same went for Refritos and Troon-Wheatley.

The latter is known to have survived by grabbing a tree root, but it might have been thought the remaining five would be killed by the drop they experienced when the floor gave way. And they would have been, had that drop stayed vertical. But, just below the site of Troon-Wheatley's life-saving tree root, the cave system angled off into a more horizontal direction. The well-like cavity became more like a giant slide in a children's playground, eventually reaching the open air and depositing the five malefactors, in a jumble of dusty limbs, at the foot of the mountain.

It took them some minutes to disentangle themselves and to get their bearings. Then General Henriquez Guiteras looked at El Chipito and El Chipito looked at General Henriquez Guiteras.

'Good heavens!' said El Chipito. 'I am meant to be meeting you in the battlefield today!'

'Good Lord,' said General Henriquez Guiteras. 'And I am meant to be meeting you in the battlefield today!'

'We must get going!' they said together.

It took the group a little while longer to work out exactly where they were. Eventually, they recognised that they'd ended up on the far side of the mountain from the Guiteras Ranch and El Chipito's encampment. And their horses were still tethered at the main entrance to the Attatotalloss Caves.

Which led to the rather incongruous sight of two men, about to engage in battle, walking side by side round a mountain.

The war did happen. Like most wars, it was bloody and inconclusive. Both sides claimed victory.

But the majority view was that the Partido Nacional Revolucionario had won. Which pleased El Chipito, who didn't want to break his record of always ending up on the winning side. Mind you, if, in the course of the war, the General's forces had shown signs of winning, El Chipito would just have gone over to their side.

Soon after the Jalapeno Province campaign finished, he headed for South America. There were always plenty of wars there that required his services. Mercenary to the end.

His forces, though, had chalked up some significant achievements in Jalapeno Province. They had cleared the Guiteras family out of their ranch and reinstated General Ignacio Contreras as governor, representing the Partido

Nacional Revolucionario. But they could not have been said to have restored peace to the region. At the end of the main hostilities, General Henriquez Guiteras had taken his surviving troops off into the mountains, where they had set up a huge, impregnable encampment. And, every time things seemed to have settled down in Jalapeño Province, they would take great delight in sallying forth on guerrilla raids and adding to the regional instability.

General Guiteras still commanded great support amongst the local peons. In their eyes, he cut a romantic figure, as opposed to the rather dour General Ignacio Contreras. As ever, the flamboyant maverick was more popular than the representative of central government. Particularly because the main activity of the government representative was collecting taxes.

Though its disruptions no longer qualified as an 'international incident', Jalapeno Province remained a Mexican trouble spot.

The outcomes for the individuals involved during Blotto and Twinks's visit to Mexico varied. As is usually the case, some were good and some were bad.

Refritos continued his work as a gangmaster, doing very little work himself but cleaning up from the labours of his peons. He also refined the design of the Refritos Grenade, so that it wouldn't detonate quite so easily in the future.

Colonel Pedro Jiminez had saved himself recriminations and punishments from General Ignacio Contreras by going over to the government side as soon as hostilities began. As a result, he was never again quite trusted by anyone. He made no attempt to rebuild his stock of black iguanas. And he continued throughout his life under the conviction, in the teeth of the evidence, that he was fatally attractive to women.

Carmelita maintained a lively and varied love-life, inviting many of the new residents to the Guiteras Ranch to share the delights of her fairy grotto. And when any of them got out of line, she didn't hesitate to give them the refried beans treatment.

On a happier romantic note, Begonia Guiteras married Carlos Contreras in a splendid ceremony in Jalapeno City. Her father was not asked to give her away and Colonel Alfredo Maldonado was not invited. Begonia had hoped that Twinks might be a bridesmaid, but her friend was long gone back to England by the time the wedding came round. The young couple had lots of children and all the happiness they deserved.

Isadora del Plato and El Falleza moved away from Jalapeno Province once the war started. She had completed her work as a multiple agent, which had been largely to sow confusion in every faction. The two of them moved on to other parts of Mexico to fulfil the obligations which were the ostensible reasons for their visit to the country, he as a bullfighter, she as a flamenco dancer.

Their relationship remained as torridly on/off as ever. And the cheaper Mexican newspapers became just as intrigued by it as the Spanish ones were.

Professor Hector Troon-Wheatley was in seventh heaven. Though he had welcomed Twinks as a helper and was glad of the heavy lifting capacity of Refritos's peons, he actually preferred doing excavations on his own. He had his own notation systems, his own filing, his own categorisation. Other people only got in the way.

And he found enough pre-Columbian history in the third level of the Attatotalloss Caves to last him a lifetime. Which in fact it did.

So nitpicky was he, so detailed in his research, that he built up more evidence than he had time to chronicle. One artefact led to another, every conclusion produced a corollary and, for someone like him, every loose end had to be followed. The prospect of his ever writing the definitive account of his findings, like the horizon, shifted ever further away. So did the prospect of wiping the complacent smiles off the faces of all those academics who had got Aztec civilisation so wrong. He found he very quickly ceased even to think about that. The research was so absorbing.

And he was left alone in the Attatotalloss Caves. After the Jalapeno Province civil war, some officials of the Partido Nacional Revolucionario came to inspect the newly revealed lowest level but, as soon as it became clear that there was none of the rumoured gold to be found there, they lost interest. Professor Hector Troon-Wheatley had the place to himself. Which is why he was in seventh heaven.

And he continued excavating and recording, without publishing anything until, many years later, he died. In the Attatotalloss Caves, of course. Leaving a twentieth-century skeleton to confuse the next archaeologist to discover his secret world.

Willy 'Ruffo' Walberswick reckoned he'd had a good war. He'd reported from the battle front and very definitely been in danger of his life. To add to that, on the eve of the conflict he'd shared moments of extreme danger and extreme passion with Estrella, the red-haired woman who would haunt his fantasies for the rest of his days. Highly satisfactory.

Ruffo was sitting in a shipping office in Veracruz, waiting to board his liner back to New York and Portsmouth and feeling extremely pleased with himself. He had finally managed to file his copy, his definitive account of the 'international incident' he had witnessed first-hand in Jalapeno Province. And that was no easy task from Mexico. Communications were primitive and he'd had to wait till he got back to Veracruz. There, his precious words had to be dictated by phone to an agency in New York, whence they would be cabled to London.

But he'd done it. He imagined the expression of delight on the face of his editor when he received this up-to-the-minute account of a conflict which he was sure no other British newspaper was covering.

His comforting reverie was broken by an accented voice, saying his name.

It was Estrella. Estrella with a large amount of luggage.

'Well, I'll be kippered like a herring!' said the astonished journalist. 'And jugged like a hare! And, come to that, battered like a pudding! Estrella! What on earth are you doing here?'

'I have come to be with you, Ruffo.'

Despair flooded through him. Hadn't the girl got it that the whole point of passion like theirs was that it was predicated on their never seeing each other again?

21

Home to Tawcester Towers

The Lagonda's journey from Mexico up through the United States to New York was uneventful. Twinks did show more interest in the sights they passed than her two male companions but, generally speaking, it was a serene and relaxed trip.

None of them felt their visit to Mexico had been wasted. Though they had had different individual experiences out there, they all shared the warm glow of knowing that, locked away in the Lagonda's secret compartment, was the Conquistadors' gold. And the supremely tasteless but extraordinarily valuable diamond-encrusted skull. The Mafia's skill in constructing the compartment ensured that they had no trouble at any of the customs posts they went through. Blotto and Corky agreed once again that it would be a bad idea to remove the compartment from the car's chassis.

Their transatlantic voyage was also without incident. Blotto didn't really miss Willy 'Ruffo' Walberswick. Twinks was just as congenial a companion in the First-Class Lounge, showing an equal capacity for the ship's Bordeaux and Hennessy Cognac.

And, during the days, while her brother was occupied

fighting off the attentions of young women who had fallen in love with him, Twinks retired to her state room and got stuck into translating *Don Quixote* from Golden Age Spanish into Etruscan.

Once their liner had docked in Portsmouth, the three travellers wasted no time in driving back in the Lagonda to Tawcester Towers.

Inevitably, the morning after their return, Blotto and Twinks were summoned to the Blue Morning Room to face the implacable eye of their mother.

'So,' said the Dowager Duchess, 'you are back.'

'Large as life,' said Blotto.

'And twice as sprauncy,' said Twinks.

'Did either of you do anything worthwhile while you were *abroad*?' She could never completely remove a shudder of distaste from that final word. Not that she ever tried to.

'It depends, Mater,' said Twinks, 'on what you mean by the word "worthwhile".'

'In your case,' came the craggy reply, 'it means did you spend the time changing your general outlook, so that next time your mother recommends someone for you to marry, you knuckle down and marry him?'

'Ah, no. Sorry, Mater. Didn't do anything that fits that particular pigeonhole.'

'If you failed to do that . . . did you, while you were *abroad* . . .' another shudder '. . . meet any wealthy foreigner prepared to marry you, keep you out there and arrange for copious amounts of money to be sent back here?'

'Another no. Sorry, Mater. Spun the cylinder to another blank there too, I'm afraid.'

'I expected as much,' the Dowager Duchess rumbled with disappointment.

There was a silence. Which Blotto decided, perhaps unwisely, to fill. 'What would you regard as "worthwhile" in my case, Mater?'

'Blotto,' she replied stentoriously, 'I have long since ceased to have any expectations of anything worthwhile from you, in any area of endeavour.'

'Ah,' said Blotto. 'Tair dibbles.'

'So, neither of you have brought back anything worth having?' the Dowager Duchess confirmed despairingly.

'Well . . .' said Twinks, 'there is the small matter of a chest of gold.'

'A chest of gold?' Their mother was instantly alert. 'How much gold?'

'On the voyage back from New York,' said Twinks, 'I borrowed some scales from the First-Class Kitchen, and I weighed all the jolly old gubbins.'

'Did you?' asked Blotto. This was news to him.

'Then, back on English soil yesterday, I got a newspaper and checked the current price of the old golden gravy.'

'So how much have we got?' demanded the Dowager Duchess, with an expression of greed that ill fitted her aristocratic status.

'Enough to deal with the Tawcester Towers plumbing for the rest of this century.'

'How much?'

Twinks leant across and whispered a number in her mother's ear.

Blotto was at first worried by the subterranean convulsion that shook his mother's face. He didn't think he'd ever seen anything like it before. Then he realised it was a smile.

A few months later, a large envelope arrived for Blotto. It contained an invitation to the wedding of 'William

200

Walberswick, son of, etc . . .' to 'Estrella Camacho, daughter of, etc . . .'. There was also a letter from Ruffo, part of which read:

'Things haven't been going too well recently on the work front. My editor rejected all the copy I sent about Jalapeno. "No one's interested in a tin-pot war in a country like Mexico." So, I'm out on my ear, end of my career as a journalist.

'But Estrella has encouraged me to buy a smallholding in Orpington, where I can grow vegetables and keep chickens . . . possibly even Buff Orpingtons, which might be rather amusing. Estrella chose Orpington because she discovered it has a thriving Women's Institute and also the schools are good.

'Oh, one thing you'll notice at the wedding is that I've given up both drinking and smoking. Estrella is of the view that they're both filthy habits and, above all things, she likes to keep a neat and tidy house . . .'

Broken biscuits, thought Blotto. It was that serious. Another good man lost to matrimony.

He needed to talk to someone about the depressing situation. He walked down to the stables. Mephistopheles would understand.